The Telltale Summer of Tina C.

D1300841

**Other APPLE® PAPERBACKS
you will want to read:**

The Chicken Bone Wish
   by Barbara Girion
The Cybil War
   by Betsy Byars
Mom, You're Fired!
   by Nancy K. Robinson
New Girl
   by Stella Pevsner
Tough-Luck Karen
   by Johanna Hurwitz
Yours Till Niagara Falls, Abby
   by Jane O'Connor

F
PeR

The Telltale Summer of Tina C.

by
Lila Perl

8245

AN
APPLE
PAPERBACK

PROPERTY OF
LA SALLE SCHOOL
MISHAWAKA, INDIANA

PB-5486

SCHOLASTIC INC.
New York Toronto London Auckland Sydney

For Lee Chupack
A wise friend and
a warm inspiration

No part of this publication may be reproduced in whole or in part, or stored in a retrieval system, or transmitted in any form or by any means, electronic, mechanical, photocopying, recording, or otherwise, without written permission of the publisher. For information regarding permission write to Houghton Mifflin Company/Clarion Books, 2 Park Street, Boston, Massachusetts 02108.

ISBN 0-590-41324-4

Copryright © 1975 by Lila Perl. All rights reserved. Published by Scholastic Inc., 730 Broadway, New York, NY 10003, by arrangement with Houghton Mifflin Company/Clarion Books. APPLE PAPER-BACKS is a registered trademark of Scholastic Inc.

12 11 10 9 8 7 6 5 4 3   0 1 2 3 4 5/9

Printed in the U.S.A.

1

Nana Tess dropped Arthur and me off at the station.

"Now listen," she said, in that crushed-gravel voice that made her sound exceptionally tough for a grandmother, "keep your eyes open for anything, *anything* at all, that seems fishy to you. Do you understand?"

We had all three gotten out of the car. Arthur stood there with his hands on his hips and his legs planted far apart. He was nine but short and padded all over with baby fat. "What do you mean? Fishy?" he wanted to know. With his eyes narrowed like that, he looked like a round-bellied dwarf.

Nana Tess made a dash for the ticket window. "Never mind," she said hoarsely over her shoulder. "Tina will know."

"Will know what?" Arthur nagged. "Why will Tina know and not me? What does 'fishy' mean? I thought you were talking to both of us."

Nana Tess kept her back to him and didn't answer until she whirled around with our two train tickets for New York City in her hand. "Arthur Carstairs," she said, bending over and looking at him threateningly, "quit whining."

"I'm not," he protested.

"He isn't," I agreed. "He only wants to know what you mean. So do I."

Nana Tess straightened up. She was no little old, shriveled grandmother. She was tall, *almost* as tall as me, but with a straight back and square shoulders, plum-red lipstick, penciled eyebrows, and short, neatly curled hair the color of stainless steel.

"Tina," she said, "don't be exasperating. There are plenty of things to watch out for and you know what they are."

If I did "know what they are," it wasn't because of anything my grandmother ever told me. Dark, mysterious hints were about all I ever got from her. So it was a lucky thing that by my thirteenth year on this planet I had found out a few things by myself. And also that last September I'd organized the Saturday Sad Souls Club where people of my age could get together and pass around information a nearly-teen-age girl needs to know to survive — and maybe even get along in this world.

Nana Tess's clickety-click dark, brown eyes were fixed on me, waiting for some kind of response. "I guess what you mean . . ." I said falteringly, "is that we shouldn't talk to anyone when we get to Penn Station and we should look around right away for Mom — for Midge, that is — to make sure she's there to meet us."

"Well, of course," she snapped. "That goes without saying. And stay close to her on the trip uptown. That neighborhood she's living in . . ." She didn't finish the sentence, just looked down at the ground and shook her head like when Arthur had spilled a whole pot of chocolate pudding on the kitchen floor because he didn't know the handle would be so hot.

Arthur's eyes lit up. "Do you think there's dope addicts up there?"

"Yes, if you must know. And other . . . things."

"Like what?" Arthur wanted to know, his interest mounting.

"Oh, like purse-snatchers," I said, trying to help out. "And drunks."

"Maybe we should've changed all our money into traveler's checks," Arthur volunteered.

"Oh, for heaven's sake!" Nana Tess said, marching us both over to the train platform, the bunch of car keys in her hand clacking against her lacquered magenta fingernails. "Let's not dramatize. New York City's dirty and noisy and dangerous enough, everybody knows that. I mean, just be sensible. I'm not always sure that your — that Midge is as careful as she ought to be. Oh, about walking into self-service elevators, for example. And after nearly a year in Mexico . . . well, that's a careless sort of place. I still can't see why she'd take an apartment on Riverside Drive, which everybody *knows* is a mugger's paradise, instead of in some nice midtown women's hotel."

Nana Tess was pacing up and down the platform with one arm around Arthur's shoulders and the other one around my waist. She wasn't really talking to *us*; she was talking out loud to herself. Ever since our mother (which was something Nana Tess never called her anymore) had come back to New York and phoned and asked to see us, Nana Tess had been nattering away like this. Mostly to our father, "poor David," as she always called him, and the rest of the time to her bridge-players and her other — mostly rich-widow-lady — friends.

As far as I was concerned, the whole problem of our broken family was getting to be a bore. It had happened nearly four years ago when Midge decided she couldn't live in suburban North Shore Long Island anymore because it just wasn't "real." She also decided that our father wasn't real and also, I guess, that Arthur and I were just a figment of somebody's imagination (not hers). I remember some of the arguments between our Mom and Pop, because I'd been listening at doorways for years. Sometimes I'd wished I was deaf; sometimes I'd even stood there listening with my fingers in my ears! In the end, Mom left and took a studio apartment in downtown Manhattan where she started painting and making wire jewelry to sell, and "poor David" sold our house and we all moved in with his mother, Nana Tess, who lived only three blocks away in an even bigger and nicer house.

So what's so terrible? We kept seeing Mom off and on. She took us to parks and playgrounds and museums. In my crowd there was nothing so unusual about your parents' being separated or divorced. Ina Philips' father had taken their baby-sitter to Disney World. The baby-sitter came back, but he didn't. He stayed in Florida and went into the citrus business. He phoned up every Friday night and he sent them a basket of grapefruit once a month like clockwork. But he still wasn't coming back, even though Ina's mother still wanted him to.

"There's the train," Nana Tess shouted. "Tina, straighten up. You're wilting again. Arthur, don't overeat no matter what kind of junk food Midge feeds you. Call me when you get there and tell me what train you're taking back tomorrow afternoon." The doors opened and she pushed us in, like the witch in *Hansel and Gretel* pushing the children into the oven.

I was hoping to be able to take off my glasses the moment we got on the train, but I knew Nana Tess would be peeking in the window until we pulled out and then would stand there waving good-by almost until we got to the next station. Wilting again . . . hmmm. Well, so would you if you were only two months past your twelfth birthday and already 5 feet, 9 inches tall — in sneakers! Pop had found a nicer way of putting it. He called me Sunflower. He said he picked that name because of those big golden heads on tall, thin stalks and the way they hung over. Only my body was also exactly like one of those tall, thin stalks. In fact, certain parts of me seemed to be totally out of control and no way to stop them, like my feet (size 9, quintuple A), my teeth (very long, too — and horsy, especially the two top front ones), and my arms ("long" sleeves usually came just below the elbow). And to make matters worse, certain *other* parts of me weren't growing at all, considering the fact that I was *practically* a teen-ager.

What if I kept on elongating until I was nothing but a pale, thin strand of spaghetti? Over and over Nana Tess would remind me that "all those gorgeous models you see are easily six feet tall." I suppose she was trying to keep me from worrying about my height. But she insisted on using that word "gorgeous," which she knew very well couldn't possibly apply to me.

Another thing that kept worrying me was what if I caught some terrible disease and all my hair fell out? It was the only *possibly* "gorgeous" thing I had — long, butterscotch blonde with sharp golden glints in it, not too straight and not too curly, not too thick and not too thin. In damp weather it frizzled out just a little and formed a sort of golden halo around my face. It was even better from the back because then you couldn't see my face. My eyes *would* have been another good feature, a sort of periwinkle blue. But I was so nearsighted I couldn't even identify my own toes without my glasses on.

Still, the moment the train began to move, I did take the stupid things off, folded them up, and wrapped them in a scarf so the plastic lenses wouldn't get scratched.

"Uh-*huh*," Arthur said smugly. "You're doing it again. I suppose now you want me to tell you if any tall, good-looking fellas come on at the next stop."

"As if you would even know one if you saw one," I replied sourly. "How would a child like you even *know* what a teen-age girl would find attractive in a man?"

"It's easy," Arthur said, leaning back into a slump and taking a package of chocolate-covered peanuts out of his pocket. He tossed a handful into his mouth. "Want some?" he mumbled through a lot of munching.

"No, they're rotten for the complexion. And fattening. Nana Tess would kill you if she saw you eating those. Especially before lunch."

Arthur ignored my remarks. "I'd know all right," he smirked. "I'd know what kind of boy you'd like. All he'd have to do would be to look like Tiger Rawson. Right?"

I blinked several times and turned stiffly to Arthur. Tiger Rawson was fifteen (well nearly) and the older brother of Arthur's best friend, Robbie. I hated Tiger ever since last week. Before that . . . well, let's just say I thought he was okay.

"See," Arthur said, "you're doing it again. Tiger was right."

"Doing what?" I demanded hotly, wrinkling my nose from side to side and then up and down. My nostrils felt all dry and pinched inside. In another moment no air would pass through them at all, I'd begin to gasp for breath, my lungs would collapse into a soft wet pulp, and I'd die.

It was a feeling that came over me whenever I got nervous or upset, before tests in school or answering out loud in class. And it was happening again — now — when

Arthur mentioned Tiger, whose nickname, by the way, suited him perfectly because he had tawny-gold hair with dark amber streaks in it, large almost fanglike white teeth, and a smug, satisfied expression like he'd just eaten up the entire population of some starving village in India.

"*It,*" Arthur said emphatically, mashing and crunching a few more chocolate peanuts between his teeth. "That telltale thing you do with your nose. The reason Tiger called you that name last Tuesday. He was dead right, too."

Arthur didn't have to say another word. I knew very well what he was talking about. From Tuesday to Saturday, you could hardly forget a thing like that. In fact, I would probably never forget it. I could still see the whole scene vividly — Ina Philips and me walking into the junior high school playground, the school we'd be going to, starting in September. Naturally we were curious about the place, about the kinds of kids who went there, what the building looked like up close, and so on. Of course, school had already closed for the summer just the Friday before, so only the playground and some of the offices and rooms on the main floor were open.

We came out of the cool, dark building into the hot, blinding-white sun of the schoolyard where a bunch of kids were tossing around a basketball. I was surprised to see Arthur and Robbie there shooting for baskets while being guarded and blocked by Robbie's brother Tiger and a few other older boys, all junior-high age. Ina and I walked over to the court so I could ask Arthur if Nana Tess knew he was there, because the school was over half a mile away from our house.

"I'm allowed to come here," Arthur had said defensively, "anytime I like." He was all hot and sweaty. "You don't have to give me any of that big-sister stuff." Arthur had the basketball in his hands and kept trying to wipe his dripping forehead. Meantime, Ina kept nudging me and poking me because Tiger was standing over near the basket. Ina is shorter than I am and definitely on the fat side. I guess we both think — thought — that Tiger was pretty terrific.

"Hey," Tiger had yelled over to Arthur. "Throw us the ball!"

Then Ina did it. She took a couple of steps forward, put her hands on her pudgy hips, leaned forward from her waist, and called back flirtatiously, "Why don't you come over here and get it?"

Tiger just grinned, showing his beautiful teeth. I could have kicked Ina. I was so embarrassed and nervous. I was sure I'd fall down in a heap if he ever did. Come over, that is. I must have started wrinkling my nose in twelve directions at once. And then, Tiger actually did start walking toward us, in a slow, catlike lope, still grinning. How stupid the two of us must have looked standing there, short, fat Ina and tall, drooping me!

Tiger didn't really know Ina, but he knew who I was on account of Robbie and Arthur's being friends. Slowly he reached over and took the basketball from Arthur and then, with I-don't-know-how-many big and smaller boys standing around, anxious to get rid of us and get on with their game, and in a voice just oozing with nastiness, he said, "Well, well, well, if it isn't Tina C., the teen-age twitch!"

Ina and I froze. Neither one of us could utter a word. A lot of the younger boys laughed out loud and the older ones just snickered, which was even worse. With that, we about-faced and walked away fast, like in a walking race. Running would have been out of the question — with Ina by my side.

That, of course, was what Arthur had

been referring to, to Tiger calling me a "twitch" last Tuesday because of that way I had of twitching my nose like a rabbit. And I don't need to tell you that I was roaring mad at Arthur for bringing it up.

The train hadn't approached the next station yet, but suddenly I yanked the box of chocolate-covered peanuts from Arthur's hand, got up out of my seat, and started marching toward the end of the car. Arthur, who was sitting near the window, jumped to his feet. "Where ya going?" His voice had a sharp note of panic in it. I kept right on walking, never looking back, and partly sliding open the door to the platform connecting our car with the next one, I threw Arthur's candy down onto the tracks. Then I returned to our seat, brushing my hands, and sat down. Somehow I'd even managed the whole operation without my glasses on.

Arthur huddled silently against the window. He was geranium red.

"If you *ever*," I said, holding my breath and talking in a hiss, "mention that word — that name that Tiger Rawson called me — or even *remind* me of it again, what just happened to those precious chocolate peanuts of yours is going to happen to you. Or something very much like it. Do you UNDER-STAND?"

Arthur's neck sank even deeper into his collar and he snuggled even closer to the smeared, dirty train window.

"And don't you dare to speak to me again until we get to Pennsylvania Station," I warned. "And then you had just better act normal. Do you understand that?"

Arthur nodded. His cheeks were still flaming and his mouth was trembling. Or was he saying something? Because just as I was turning away from him to look straight ahead of me in still-throbbing anger, I could have sworn I saw his lips move and form a single word — "twitch!"

2

We came off the elevator into a dim, echoing hallway with cracked tile flooring and a smell of stale cooked vegetables.

"Pee-yoo!" Arthur exclaimed, grabbing for his nose. "What's that terrible smell?"

Midge — our mother — was walking in front of us toward one of the apartment doors. They were all painted very dark green and chipped and scarred, with dirty, lighter-colored paint showing through.

"Last month's cauliflower, last week's broccoli. Things like that," she said lightly, half over her shoulder.

Midge didn't seem as tall to me as a year ago. She was still thin, though, in jeans and sneakers, with a checked cotton shirt tucked in and the sleeves rolled up to her elbows. Her hair, just about the color of mine but straighter and thicker, was in a long tight braid down her back. She was wearing wire-frame eye-glasses, no makeup. She hadn't changed really at all, and she never would have passed inspection at the Saturday Sad Souls Club. I could just imagine Ina and Amy and Cokie going to work on her with suggestions from *Teen Charm* and other magazines. With all her possibilities, she was a perfect "before" for remaking into a really fantastic "after."

Arthur was still holding his nose, while Midge fumbled with the locks on the door. "Don't they ever cook anything else around here?" he wanted to know. "What are they, vegetarians?" His voice came out high-pitched and distorted because of his tightly pressed-together nostrils.

Nobody answered. Two locks clicked and a heavy chain fell down and clattered against the inside of the door.

16

"Hey," Arthur said, forgetting about his nose. "That's keen. How'd you do that?"

"It's easy," Midge replied. "Watch again." She reached in and hooked up the inside chain, which locked into place.

"You mean," Arthur said, "even if I broke open the two outside locks, I still couldn't get in because of that chain on the inside?"

"Right. Unless you had the key for the chain box." She handed Arthur the key, and he reached up and poked his wrist in, straining a little, fitted the key into the top of the box, turned it, and again the chain fell out through the bottom.

"Guess you get plenty of robbers coming around here," he remarked, trying to sound very man-of-the-world. "That is, if they can stand the smell in the hallway while they're busting open the locks."

We both followed Midge into the apartment. There was a long, dark corridor leading straight ahead, with a row of tiny rooms opening off it to the left. Arthur swung down the corridor, peering into each one, as though he was starting out on some great adventure. "What do you know!" he exclaimed. "It's just like a railway train with compartments for the passengers to sit in. Like in those foreign mystery movies where people disappear all the time. This place is keen. I like it."

I wished Arthur wouldn't get so enthusiastic. Frankly, I thought the place was disgusting. It was just as plain and ugly as the way Midge dressed and looked. Except I suppose there wasn't much anyone could do to improve an old dump of a building like this. But Mom could have looked lots better. I'd seen her wedding photo once, when Nana Tess was cleaning out drawers and closets. She looked like a bride's-magazine model, in a long white satin dress with a veil edged in orange blossoms, her hair parted in the center and two honey-smooth blonde cascades coming down over her shoulders resting on either side of her chest. Scrumptious! No glasses. Violet-blue eyes. A dreamy smile, her lips slightly parted. Her nose was definitely smaller than mine, her front teeth shorter. She even had a chest. Just about the size I was hoping for. Only where was it now? On the real Midge, I mean? You couldn't tell anything from that loose, oversize shirt she had on.

By this time Arthur had reached the living room at the far end of the hall, and he was already lifting the window and shrieking. "Zowie! Hey, Teen, come look! The river, lots of boats, and up that way — hey, what do you know — the George Washington Bridge."

"Take it easy," I said. "You'll fall out." Mom laughed, went up behind him, and raised the window a little higher. "It's okay," she said. "He can't."

There was a rusty iron grating outside that curved around in a semicircle from one side of the window frame to the other. You couldn't really call it a balcony; it was more of a basket. We were up on the sixth floor and the view was pretty good. That is, if you also liked peering across the Hudson at New Jersey, which was belching smoke as though it was trying hard to hide the whole rest of the country from view.

"Phew!" I said, wrinkling my nose madly from side to side, although this was one time I would have preferred my nostrils sealed rather than open. "Talk about broccoli and cauliflower. This is the real thing, the pollution that kills. I honestly wouldn't breathe out there, Arthur, if I were you."

I turned back into the living room. It was by far the largest room in the apartment and furnished with things that could only have come from a couple of dozen garage sales. There was an overstuffed sofa that looked like a tired, worn-out version of the kind of upholstered furniture Nana Tess gave away every few years, apologizing for its "disgraceful condition." Then there were some chairs made out of narrow metal tubing and bright-colored canvas that looked like pool-terrace furniture, and there was a table that looked like a barrel standing on one end. (The reason it looked that way was that it really was a barrel.)

Midge also had some pieces of wicker and woven straw that maybe came from Mexico, and a big scarlet, purple, and green woolen cloth tacked to the wall above the sofa that I think was called a *serape*, something you were supposed to wear, if you were a Mexican. On the other wall there were two large bullfight posters announcing the names of the matadors and dates that were long since over. By now the bulls were all dead and some of the matadors had probably been gored in the stomach.

"Well," Mom said coming back into the room with two glasses of Coke. "Let's sit down and catch up on old times a little. We'll have lunch pretty soon now." Arthur pulled back in from the window ledge, not too willingly, and we both sat down on the sofa.

Midge drew up a low wicker stool with a bright orange cushion on it.

We three had hardly said anything to one another on the subway ride rattling uptown from Penn Station. The noise the train made, especially with all the windows open blowing in dirty hot air, was just terrific. No wonder everybody in New York City yelled in the street, instead of talking quietly to one another. They probably thought they were still on the subway.

We got on the usual subject of school. That was always safe for openers. It turned out Mom hadn't gotten about half of our letters written to her in Mexico because she'd been moving around quite a bit. But we'd gotten all her post cards. Arthur had them in a box at home. He was especially fascinated with the pyramids, with hundreds of steep steps and no banisters.

The conversation came to a dead stop. Sure enough, it was twenty minutes before twelve. Did you ever notice that whenever a whole roomful of people gets dead silent, it's always either twenty minutes before the hour or twenty minutes past? The only noise in the room came from Arthur who was crunching on a piece of ice he'd dug out from the bottom of his empty Coke glass.

"So . . ." I began, trying to look directly at Midge, which I always found hard to do because I never felt sure about what her relationship was to me. She wasn't a mother, really; she wasn't even a mother-type. She was more of a big sister or a young aunt, but she wasn't quite that either. I was a lot more comfortable with Ina Philips' mother, for example, in spite of her fussy habits and her self-conscious chatter, chatter, chatter; and, of course, Nana Tess was as comfortable as an old shoe, even when she was giving me a hard time. "So," I started up again, figuring somebody had better say something, "how did you like Mexico?"

"It was good," Midge replied quickly, smoothing her hair and tucking it back more firmly behind her ears with her long, bony fingers. Maybe she was a little ill at ease with us, too. I felt sorry for her, and I didn't like feeling that way. It made me even more uncomfortable. "Real good. Until I got sick, anyway. After that, it was all downhill. I stuck it two more months, and then I knew I had to come back to New York. Anyhow, I really got to missing you two. . . ." Her voice trailed off. Nobody said anything. "But I did some good work down there," she said, her voice growing louder and more cheerful again. "I picked up some fabulous ideas for jewelry designs, and I sculpted, and I began to get really interested in pottery."

Arthur suddenly found his tongue. "What kind of sickness did you get?" He had a morbid interest in diseases of all kinds. Pop said he was setting up a special education trust fund so Arthur could be a doctor without fail.

Mom smiled. "I don't know if you ever heard of it. It's called Montezuma's revenge."

"What's it come from?" Arthur demanded. "Did you get thrown off the top of a pyramid or something?"

"Oh, Arthur," I groaned. "Honestly. They don't throw people off the tops of pyramids anymore. That was centuries ago. Anyhow, they used to tear out their victims' hearts first. If that *had* happened to Mom, she'd have been dead anyway before she hit the bottom." I stopped myself. I didn't mean to get so carried away. But that Arthur . . .

Mom meantime was rocking back and forth on her footstool and laughing hard, the first real belly laughing I'd seen her do all day. Her feet came so far up off the ground that I thought she was going to flip over backward. Then she leaned forward and hugged

Arthur until he turned a fiery red. Well, at least it broke the ice.

"No," Mom said, recovering at last. "Nothing like that. Montezuma's revenge is caused by a bug of some kind. Gets to your intestines and gives you severe diarrhea. They say it's a curse placed by the Indians on the white man ever since the Spaniards invaded the empire of the Aztecs. But I guess you studied all about that in school."

"Not yet," Arthur said soberly. "But I know all about it anyway. Tell you what you ought to do, though. You ought to try that stuff called *Kao* . . . *Kaopecter* . . . something like that. You can get it in a drugstore, no prescription necessary. I'll ask Nana Tess and find out the exact . . ."

We all stopped dead again. And it wasn't twenty to *or* twenty after. Naturally, it was always awkward talking to Mom about Nana Tess or Pop, and vice versa.

Midge cleared her throat. "How is Nana Tess anyway?" You could see she was trying to sound politely interested.

But before either one of us could answer, there was a loud noise at the door of the apartment, sort of a thud, followed by the sound of locks being fiddled with.

Arthur jumped off the sofa with a start.

"Uh-oh! Here they come. It's the robbers for sure. Hey, the chain, the chain! We didn't put back the chain." And he made as if to start down the hall, both fists clenched, but waiting for Mom to go with him because you could see he was scared.

To our surprise, though, Midge just sat there quietly. She didn't look alarmed in the least. "It's okay," she said. "It's only Peter."

Arthur, almost in the entryway where the long corridor connected with the living room, unfroze from his position. "Who's *that?*" he asked, not particularly expecting an answer. He was uncertain whether to come back to the sofa and sit down or not, but he finally did.

Meantime we could hear both locks being unlocked, the door being opened, and a voice that sounded like that of an older boy — much older — older even than Tiger Rawson, called out, "Hi! Ahoy in there. Be with you in a minute."

There were sounds of footsteps and heavy rustling, and a clicking noise, almost like knitting needles going fast. Gosh, that was a long hall. Midge could see whoever was coming before we could because she was facing that way. She looked up with a friendly, calm smile, and we followed her glance.

A young man came into the room, medium-height and of fairly stocky build, with smooth, thick brown hair, a rather full face, and wire-rimmed eyeglasses. In his arms were two large brown-paper bags of groceries and behind him trotted a worried-looking dog, its head down and its short, black-and-brown fur heavily speckled with gray.

"Hello," said the young man, drawing out the "o" like he was really pleased to meet us and it was about time, too. "Tina and Arthur. Nice to know you both. I'm Peter."

We nodded in unison and mumbled something that (I hoped) sounded like "Pleased to meet you." Mom looked back and forth from Peter to us with big eyes. The dog finally lifted its head and said something that sounded like "Ruhf!" He was medium-sized with a jutting lower jaw, a short beard, and an honest-to-goodness wrinkled forehead. He must have been a mixture of a dozen or more different breeds but mostly, I would have said, schnauzer.

"Take it easy," Peter said to the dog. "We're all friends here."

26

"What's his name?" Arthur wanted to know.

"Wart," Peter replied.

"Why? Does he have warts?" Arthur asked. "I never heard of a dog having warts, but if he does, I know a good cure for them. You get this stuff. You can get it at the drugstore, no prescription necess . . ."

Mom reached forward and put a hand on Arthur's knee. "No. No warts. His real name is Worrywart. Because he has this hard job taking care of people and he worries about it a lot. So we call him Wart, for short. See?"

Arthur nodded. "Oh. It's a good name. Hey, Wart, come 'ere, boy."

Peter heaved a sigh of mock relief. "Okay. Now that that's settled, excuse me while I go and get these grocery bags unloaded."

I watched Peter go out of the room. "We?" I said to Midge. "Is he your dog or Peter's dog?"

"Both," Mom said, matter-of-factly. But I could see her eyes on me, carefully watching my face. "Peter lives here, too."

"Oh," I said, already guessing he did because he had a set of keys. "You mean he shares the apartment. I suppose he helps out with the rent."

Mom nodded. "Well, let's just say he helps

out. We help each other out. I'm working full-time again, you know. At a designer's studio downtown. It's interesting and challenging, but it's a long day. By the time I get home at night, I'm bushed. And I'm trying to set up a line of my own handmade jewelry on the side."

Arthur wasn't paying any attention. He was sitting on the floor stroking Wart and mumbling things to him. The dog wasn't unfriendly, but he wasn't jumping all over Arthur either. He just stood near him like they were having a casual conversation. As for me, I was getting more and more confused, and besides I was starting to get awfully hungry. A few more minutes and my stomach would be challenging Wart to a growling contest. I wondered why Mom just kept sitting there watching Arthur and Wart. Why didn't she get up and go in the kitchen, help Peter empty the grocery bags, and start making lunch? I thought maybe I should offer to help her just to give her the idea and get her started.

Just then Peter popped his head around the doorway. "Lunch in five minutes," he announced, "honest to goodness. That's just time enough for all you guys to get started washing up."

"Oh, good!" Mom said, jumping up from her stool like a little girl, pigtail bouncing. "I'm starved. What are we having?"

Peter took a couple of steps into the room. He clicked his heels together and bowed. "French toast sandwiches, madame, stuffed with baked sliced Virginia ham and melted Gruyère cheese; crisp, raw celery and carrot sticks; sliced beefsteak tomatoes; and for dessert — hot fudge sundaes, prepared of course with my own inimitable creamy-smooth, super-rich, extra-chocolaty, home-made, hot fudge sauce."

Arthur's head shot up like a bullet. "Hot fudge! Oh, boy, that's my favorite. Did you know around my way they call me the hot fudge kid? Honest. It's my name! Ask any-one." He turned to me. "Right, Teen?"

"Right," I said wearily.

Peter turned and Arthur followed him toward the kitchen, still talking about how much he liked hot fudge sauce and anything chocolate in general. Mom followed Peter and Arthur, and Wart followed Mom. "Come on, Arthur," Mom was saying. "Give Peter a few minutes to get the food on the table, and meantime I'll show you where the bath-room is so you can get washed up."

I stood up and looked around me in the

empty room. Outside the window, New Jersey was still belching smoke, and the George Washington Bridge, looping high across the river, looked like it didn't care. I shrugged my shoulders. Was anybody around here normal? Arthur, the chocolate nut; a dog who acted like he was somebody's worried old grandfather; a man who did all the shopping and cooking around the house; and Mom who wasn't interested in anything but her work.

Mom in particular. No wonder I had to keep on reminding myself who she was.

3

The Saturday Sad Souls Club met on Wednesday. It was our first meeting in two and a half weeks. Graduations, end-of-school, and going-away parties had been taking up the past couple of weekends, and we were short one member because Cokie Adams had gone off to camp. Also, last Saturday had been Arthur's and my visit to Midge.

The meeting was held at our house in the basement den. Of course, that led to a "discussion" with Nana Tess who couldn't see why we didn't hold it on the pool terrace and have a swimming party at the same time.

"Since you girls are so interested in beauty and in improving your looks," Nana Tess remarked pointedly, "I can't see why you would deny your complexions the benefits of good fresh air."

"For the simple reason," I replied, "that the sun is very bad for the skin. Especially mine. I'd rather be milky white than lobster red. And anyhow these meetings are private."

Nana Tess sniffed. "As if I'd even peek. I've got twenty much more important things to do this afternoon. At *least*. But suit yourself."

That's just what I'll do, I thought secretly, even though "suit yourself" from Nana Tess always meant "you're making a big mistake."

Arthur was blessedly away, swimming over at Robbie Rawson's pool. Ina was the first to arrive. She had walked the five blocks and looked damp and pasty, but not thinner. I gave her a glass of tomato, green pepper, and cucumber juice made in the blender at the denroom bar, with lots of ice and plenty of salt in it.

Ina heaved herself onto one of the bar

stools and drank it rapidly. "I was beginning to wonder if we were going to have any meetings at all this summer," she panted, putting down the drained glass and reaching for a pretzel.

"Pretzels are a no-no," I warned her. "I put them out for Amy, not for you."

"Just one." She swiveled, hooked her feet on the rungs of the stool, and leaned back against the bar. "So how was your mother?"

"The same," I said. "Hopelessly drab. She doesn't care a thing about her looks." We were supposed to tell each other everything in the SSSC, but I wasn't about to start spilling the whole story about Peter and Wart and the apartment. For some reason, which Arthur and I had never discussed, we hadn't even mentioned Peter to Nana Tess.

Ina clicked her tongue against the roof of her mouth in disapproval. "Mine, of course, is too much the other way now. Did you know she was starting dating?"

"No," I said, surprised, although why should I have been? "Who with?"

"Some man," Ina murmured indifferently. "He looked old. Much older than my dad. No Tiger Rawson, I can tell you."

"Now, why'd you have to bring that up?" I asked her, turning hot and my nostrils

33

already beginning to feel a little dry and itchy.

"Well, I still think he's cute. Even if he did call you . . ."

"Never mind what he called me," I said snappishly. "Arthur already reminded me of that and he got his."

"Okay, okay," Ina soothed. "Only just remember the 'teen-age' part. He could have just said 'Tina C., the blank.' But he did say, 'Tina C., the teen-age blank.' Didn't you think that part at least was flattering? After all, you might be in your thirteenth year, but it's still a long way to your thirteenth birthday. How would he know that? So probably you looked like a regular teen-ager to him."

I thought about that a moment. "No, it wasn't flattering, not combined with the other name he called me. Listen, let's not talk about it anymore."

Ina shrugged. "Okay." On the whole she was a pretty good friend. "Where's Amy anyway?"

"Late," I said. "What else? Or she forgot altogether."

Like speaking of the devil, the next moment there was an uneven clattering of footsteps coming down the basement stairs and

Amy appeared, looking breathless and confused. Her ragged, thin brown hair, which had recently been cut in a gamin style by one of the most expensive hair stylists on the North Shore, was shooting out in all directions and had parted itself in the front exposing her too-high forehead. What with her eyeglasses on crooked, her shirt buttoned into the wrong buttonholes, and her jeans sagging she looked like — well, she looked like Amy.

"Don't say a word. I'm late. I know it," she gasped. "But there's a reason." She stepped to one side and beckoned to someone or something on the staircase behind her. Whatever it was, was hidden from us by the wood-paneled stairway wall. "Look!"

A pretty redheaded girl instantly appeared, like a magician's assistant, at Amy's side, her face lit up with a friendly smile revealing perfect teeth (no braces), crinkly brown eyes with long red-gold lashes (no glasses), and a just-about-perfect figure. She was wearing brown corduroy shorts and a pale shell-pink, sleeveless turtleneck top with deep cutout armholes.

"I'm Karla," she said. She could have been an airline stewardess, except of course she was around our age, probably twelve or twelve-and-a-half.

"Karla Hunt," Amy said proudly.

"Hi, Karla." I spoke very coolly, I must admit. Ina waggled her fingers at Karla, nodded and smiled, and said, "Hi." What now, I thought? She can't stay for the meeting. We were late starting as it was, so there was no other way but to come right out and say it.

"Look," I began slowly, "it's really nice to meet you, Karla. I'm Tina and this is Ina. I guess you know." Karla nodded, her thick, shining auburn hair bouncing wildly and falling back into place beautifully. "But this is a private club and we're having a closed meeting. I don't know if Amy told you that." I glared pointedly at Amy.

"Of course, of course," Amy gushed. "Karla understands. I explained all that. But don't you see, she has a good reason for being here. She just moved into the Raymonds' house, the one they sold last month — next door to us — and I'm proposing her for a new member."

"I see," I said, wishing Ina would say something to Karla instead of just staring at her openmouthed and leaving it all to me. She'd been quick enough to say something to

Tiger Rawson just when she should never have opened her mouth.

"Well, it's like this, Amy," I went on, "and you should know the rules. First, we have to have our regular meeting and that's closed to nonmembers. Definitely. Then, near the end under New Business, we have to take up the question of admitting a new member, have a discussion about it, and have the voting. She can't be present then, either. So Karla would have to wait around an awfully long time upstairs . . ."

"Oh, I don't mind," Karla said quickly. Her voice was both squeaky and exuberant. "I could take a swim in the pool, maybe. If you don't mind, that is. I've got my bikini on under this." Her thumbs flew to the armholes of the shell-pink turtleneck and stretched them forward in case we wanted to look. "See, our house is a terrible mess because we only just moved in day before yesterday. And the pool's all drained and dirty. The Raymonds never filled it up this year because they knew they were moving out. . . ."

"Is it okay, then, Tina?" Amy asked anxiously. I looked at Ina. She was still staring at Karla in spellbound admiration. But she managed to move her head up and down in agreement, like a sleepwalker.

"Sure," I said, even though my heart wasn't in it. Because otherwise we'd never get on with the meeting. "It's okay. Just go on in. Oh, and if you see a lady up there, it's my grandmother. She'll give you anything you want, a cool drink, show you where the towels are. Just tell her I said it's okay."

Karla squealed and clapped her hands. "Oh, thank you, thank you! You're all too kind. I love it here already. I just know I'm going to adore being a member of the club." And she whirled around and ran up the stairs.

Amy fell into a chair as though she was exhausted. "What's wrong?" she said guiltily, trying to avoid what I hoped was my iciest blue stare. "Tell me what I did wrong. There's no rule that says we can't have new members. We don't have too many now. With Cokie away for the summer, there are only three of us. That isn't hardly enough for a meeting."

"You know very well what's wrong," I hissed. *"Nothing* is wrong. Nothing is the least *bit* wrong with Karla 'I've-got-my-bikini-on' Hunt! And, Ina, I wish you'd come out of that fog you're in and say something."

Ina snapped to attention at last. "Tina's right," she said. "She's gorgeous."

"I don't know about 'gorgeous,'" I remarked sourly, "but attractive enough. You seem to have forgotten the whole idea of this club, Amy. It's not for stewardess-type redheads with twenty-twenty vision and great legs. It's for people like — like us. With problems concerning their looks and their personalities, people who would like to become more . . . popular. Do I have to remind you what SSSC stands for?" I paused, hoping my words were sinking in. "Okay, forget the first S. I know it's Wednesday."

Amy leaned forward fingering a pretzel and sipping the sugar-free Seven-Up I'd handed her (her waistline was okay but the sugar was bad for her spotty complexion). "But there *is* something wrong with Karla," she said earnestly. "Couldn't you see? No, I guess you couldn't. The light's pretty dim down here."

We both looked at Amy in anticipation.

"So you didn't notice anything at all? That's odd. Well, she's covered with freckles. Millions of them. Her face, arms, legs — all over her. I mean *all* over. Everywhere."

"You idiot," Ina burst out. "They're gorgeous! Didn't you know? Freckles are *in*."

Amy looked stricken. She appealed to me with her eyes. "Are they? Really?"

"Of course, they are," I said drily. "If you paid any attention to the things you ought to, you'd know that. Some of the most popular young actresses on the screen today are covered with freckles."

"And the makeup men don't do a thing to hide them," Ina chimed in. "They could, of course, if they wanted to. They could make their skins look as smooth as cream. But they don't. Because one thing no makeup artist can do is *give* somebody freckles if they don't have them. And they *are* in."

Amy sank back. She looked beaten. She took off her glasses and wiped them with a moist tissue. Pieces of the tissue began to curl up and fall into her lap. "Well, in that case" — she started hesitantly — "I didn't want to have to tell you, but there *is* something else. Only it's very serious. And you can't see it by looking at her. It's — well, it's something she does."

Ina and I stared at Amy. "Something she does?"

"Right. Something dangerous. Only she can't help herself. She says she's tried. But it's like an emotional thing — a — a hang-up. A sickness really. Nobody on earth's supposed to know. Her parents don't know. She told me only in the strictest confidence. But I guess I'll have to tell you."

I was beginning to get awfully nervous and impatient. "All right," I said. "Enough already. Tell."

Amy put her glasses back on. There were shreds of white tissue caught between the lenses and the frames and one clinging smack in the center of her left eyepiece.

"She steals," she said, barely speaking the second word.

There was a moment of utter silence.

"Steals? Steals what?" Ina demanded, but softly.

"Anything. Anything small that she can lift off the counter and get away with easily."

"You mean she shoplifts," I said sternly.

Amy gulped and nodded. "Yup. All kinds of stuff."

"How do you know?" Ina leaned forward on the bar stool. "I mean, what proof do you have?"

We were all three whispering by now.

"She showed me," Amy retorted. "She keeps all the stuff in boxes, hidden away in her room — pencils, erasers, ball points, felt tips, paper clips, rubberbands, rolls of Scotch tape. . . ."

"Why stuff like that?" Ina asked. "Doesn't she ever take anything else, like eyeliner or nail polish? Nothing from the makeup counter?"

"Yes, she does. That, too. But mostly it's stuff from the stationery counter. She says she doesn't know why. That's part of her sickness."

"Doesn't she use any of the things she takes? Does she keep all of it hidden away in boxes like that?" Ina asked.

"Just about all," Amy replied. "That's part of her sickness, too."

"Well, that settles it," I exclaimed, slapping my hand down hard on the bar. Everybody jumped. "Who wants her in the club? We'd be crazy to take her in. Suppose she got caught? She'd bring disgrace on all of us. The police would probably come and investigate her friends. Forget it. She's out!"

"Wait a minute, Tina," Amy shrilled. "I didn't tell you the whole thing. She isn't going to do it anymore. That's why she wants to join the club. She feels that if she has some good friends and can be happy out here, she won't have the temptation to go shoplifting anymore. She moved here from the city, see? Her family was living in this tall, expensive apartment building on the upper East Side. And the kids she was going with were all from well-off families and they all used to go around to the five-and-tens and take things. Just for kicks. She had to do it, too, or she wouldn't have had any friends at all. And then it sort of got to be a habit that she couldn't break."

"That only goes to show she has a very weak character," I said coldly.

"For heaven's sake, Tina," Amy urged, "don't you have *any* human sympathy?" She turned to Ina. "What do you think? Couldn't we give her a chance? Take her in on a temporary basis, say for three months? If she does anything bad, she's out. If not, she stays. We'd be doing her a good turn, don't you see? Isn't that the purpose of the club? To help each other?"

I could see Ina weakening. "Well, if you put it that way..."

"Karla," I mused softly to myself, "Karla the Kleptomaniac."

"Now don't be mean," Ina cautioned.

"Why not?" I said. "Other people are." I guess I was thinking of what Tiger Rawson had called me. In fact, I still couldn't get it out of my mind. Why was it all right for me to be hurt all the time, while everybody else was supposed to be treated with kindness and consideration?

"That's true," Ina suddenly agreed. She must have been thinking the same thing. "But maybe if . . . hey, maybe if we *all* had secret club names like that one, like Karla the Kleptomaniac, just among ourselves of course, we'd watch out for our faults better and we could correct them."

"Like what?" asked Amy. "You mean, like Amy the Amnesiac? That's what my father always calls me. Because I'm always late or forgetting things or losing things."

"Or buttoning your·blouse crooked or getting pieces of tissue all over your eyeglasses and in your lap and never even noticing," I added. "In fact, I think you just ate one."

We all burst out laughing.

"What would *my* secret club name be?" Ina wondered. "Ina the Fat?"

"No," I said, thinking hard. "That isn't right. It has to be an — alliteration. Remember, we learned about that in sixth-grade poetry? All the important words have to start with the same letter."

"Oh, I know what you mean," Amy shouted. "You mean something like . . . like Ina the Insomniac!"

"Right," I said. "Only wrong. That's some-body who can't sleep and stays up all night. That's no good for Ina."

Ina jumped off the stool. "But it is. It's right! That *is* me. I do stay up all night. Well, not *all* night, but I get up in the middle, you know. I always do. Ever since my dad moved away — to Florida. Mom leaves the lights on all night, and I go downstairs to the re-frigerator and have a midnight snack. I know I shouldn't, but I do. Do you want to know what I had last night? Well, it was about 1:30, and there was this leftover egg salad from lunch, just oozing with mayon-naise, and some strips of fried bacon and this delicious, fresh onion-pumpernickel bread — "

"Enough!" I cried. "Stop this minute. And to think I waste my time making you ten-calorie vegetable-juice drinks in the blender. You ought to be ashamed."

But Ina seemed delighted. "So that's my name then, huh? I like it. Ina the Insomniac, Amy the Amnesiac, Karla the Kleptomaniac, Tina the . . . Tina the what?"

"Okay, okay," I said. "I get the idea. I guess it's got to be Tina the . . . the . . ."

"Tina, the Teen-Age Twitch?" Ina offered gently.

"Why?" asked Amy. Ina hadn't told her then. I was relieved about that. As I said, Ina was a pretty good friend. I twitched my nose for Amy just to remind her.

"Oh, yeah," she said, "you're always doing that. Well, maybe not always. I think it tells when you're nervous or scared. It's a terrible habit. You really ought to break it."

I looked down at Amy's feet in torn, dirty white sneakers. "Do you think I'll get around to breaking it before or after you remember to put on both socks?" I teased her.

Amy looked down in confusion. "Oh, gee, I couldn't find the other one," she protested. "And I was late. Something's always missing everywhere I turn. I guess I just have no memory. Okay, okay, I know wearing only one sock looks dumb."

"It is dumb," I agreed.

Of course, there was no time to hold a regular full-length meeting that afternoon. So I just called the meeting to order, skipped over Old Business, skipped over Regular Business (reports on Beauty Tips, Diets, Family Problems, Hobbies and Recreation, and What To Do About Boys), and went on to New Business. Under New Business it was resolved: 1) that each club member should henceforth have a *secret, alliterative* club name, and 2) that Karla Hunt should become a probationary member, for a three-month trial period, of the Saturday Sad Souls Club. Both motions were carried unanimously.

"What are we going to do about Cokie?" Ina asked. "I mean about a name for her. We can't call her Cokie the Camper."

"No, of course not," I said. "That's only *where* she is, not *what* she is. We'll think of something, though, before the next meeting." I turned to Amy. "Okay, call Karla down here and tell her our decision. Of course it goes without saying, she has to accept all the conditions. Including her club name."

Amy jumped up. "Oh, I'm sure she will," she said happily. "Karla's really very easy to get along with. You'll see."

After Amy left, I turned to Ina. "I hope we made the right decision," I said.

"I'm sure we did," she replied. "She's probably got lots of good beauty tips. I'd love to know how she keeps her hair that way."

"I didn't mean that," I confessed. "I meant about the secret names. Even in the club here, just among ourselves, it's somehow awful to say it. Tina the Teen-Age . . . Twitch."

"There," Ina said comfortingly. "You've said it. Don't you feel better now that it's out?"

"No," I answered, feeling my color rising and my nostrils going dry again. "It still makes me miserable. And I *know* I'm not going to like telling it to Karla."

4

It was Saturday morning and I was sitting on the pool terrace under the big umbrella writing a letter to Cokie Adams; poor Cokie, the only one of us SSSC members who had gotten herself shunted off to camp this summer. How the rest of us managed to avoid it was something of a miracle. Well . . . that, and a little common sense.

Amy and I both told our families that our counsellors the summer before had smoked grass (which wasn't even a lie), and Ina had gotten out of it because her mother had to cut down on expenses until the alimony and child-support arrangements with her escaped father were settled. But Cokie's parents, who were just getting *together* again *after* a separation, had their hearts set on a trip to Scandinavia, so Cokie was doomed.

"Anyhow, I hope you won't mind," I wrote Cokie, after telling her all about Karla and the Wednesday meeting, "having a secret club name like the rest of us. If you have any other ideas write and tell us before the next meeting, but my own suggestion would be Cokie the Curvature."

I was sorry about that, but she was a Sad Soul like the rest of us and the name was very appropriate. Cokie had braces on her teeth, a part-time posture brace on her back because her spine curved a little, and even arch supports in her shoes. Everything on her seemed to curve too much or too little and never in the right direction. But even though she was so full of correctional devices for the present, I was sure Cokie would turn out all right. She had dark blonde hair, an olive-toned complexion, a snub nose, and sea-green eyes. And the camp she was at was coed.

I was just ending my letter with, "So what are the boys like up there this summer? You never said. Creeps, I'll bet," when Pop came strolling onto the terrace.

He was just back from tennis, dressed in white shorts and still swinging a racket. His legs, as well as the rest of him, were gorgeously tanned, and his smooth, regular features wore a pleasant smile.

"Hello, Sunflower," he said casually, kissing the top of my head. "Which good-looking boyfriend are you writing to now?"

"No boyfriend," I said, annoyed. I hated it when Pop made jokes like that.

Pop sat down opposite me in one of the low plastic sling chairs. "Rosebud's here," he remarked. "She's in the house, changing. Going to take a swim before lunch."

"Oh," I said, folding up Cokie's letter. "Is she staying to lunch?"

Pop nodded. "Um hmmm."

Rosebud was Pop's tennis partner. At least, he'd met her at the club and they'd been playing together quite a lot all spring and summer. She was a Hungarian refugee, but a rich one, always talking about her Swiss bank account. Arthur and I sometimes imitated her accent, which I know was mean. But she had a high-pitched voice and called everybody "d-a-a-r-r-r-ling," and seemed like a very silly person all around, especially when she threw back her carefully tousled blonde head and laughed with her mouth wide open as if she were never going to stop.

It was on one of these occasions that Arthur had noticed she didn't have a single filling in her teeth. In fact, he'd even gone and stood right in front of her, peering into her mouth, which made her stop laughing very suddenly, sit bolt upright, and snap her lips together like a trap. But Arthur had seen enough. "No cavities in a person that old?" he later remarked to me. "Impossible! She's got false teeth. I'd bet my new ten-speeder on it."

Well, maybe she did and maybe she didn't. Who knows what her parents fed her when she was a child in Hungary. Maybe crunchy raw vegetables and hard black bread, and no candy or soft drinks ever. I never really thought much about her. Or even how old she was. Over twenty and under forty were about the same thing to me.

I wrote Cokie's name and camp address on the outside of the envelope. Pop shifted his position in his chair. The racket was now resting across his knees. "You know, you never really told me, Sunflower, how you enjoyed your visit to the city last week."

I glanced up. "You mean seeing Mom?"

Pop nodded, lifted the racket for a moment, and crossed his legs so one ankle rested on the opposite knee. Why did he always have to politely beat around the bush instead of coming out and saying exactly what he meant?

"It was okay," I said, licking the envelope flap generously back and forth several times. The paste on it had a sort of custardy flavor. Not bad.

"Just okay? Weren't you happy to see her again?"

"Sure," I said. "Arthur and I were both happy. I guess."

Pop cleared his throat. "How'd you think she looked? Has she changed much?"

Why was he asking all these questions? Pop's conversations were usually just a lot of amiable nothings. He never seemed to have any strong opinions about anything. He seldom scolded, so his praises always seemed a little meaningless. Maybe all he wanted was for everybody to like him. I once heard him say, in an argument with Mom when they were still together, that the last thing he wanted to do was to "rock the boat."

Maybe the reason she had found him so "unreal" had something to do with that. Maybe it even had something to do with the kind of work he did. It was called investment banking and it sounded very dry and colorless.

"Well," I said, smoothing my fingers back and forth across the pasted-down envelope flap, "I didn't think she looked too good. Kind of thin and pale. She got this disease in Mexico. Montezuma's revenge, it's called. Arthur was very interested."

Pop laughed. "Yes, he would be, young Dr. Carstairs. What an M.D. that kid's going to make!" His laughter died, and his face became serious. "I thought she looked peaked, too. I think she'll start picking up again now she's back home, though."

"You?" I said, surprised. "When did you see her? I didn't know you two . . ."

"I saw her Thursday evening when I stayed in town after the office for a couple of hours."

Pop suddenly lifted the tennis racket straight up in front of him like a stop signal. My face must have shown some sign of hope that maybe, after all . . .

"Uh-oh. No, nothing like that, Sunflower," Pop said quickly. "Sorry. She made her choice and she's sticking with it. I thought you knew she got the divorce while she was in Mexico."

"No," I said sullenly. "I didn't know. Nobody tells me anything around here. Except what I should do and shouldn't do, where I should go and shouldn't go. They're very good at telling me things like that."

Pop leaned forward, his brow wrinkling with concern, and put a warm hand on my knee. "I'm sorry about that, Tina love. I guess she and I didn't get our signals straight about who was going to tell you and Arthur about that. Anyhow, the divorce is final. She's got some pretty strong ideas, that girl."

I wriggled in my chair. It was always uncomfortable talking about these things. If my parents had problems, let them worry. It was bad enough they weren't behaving like real parents were supposed to, being a typical mother and father to Arthur and me, presenting a united front and acting like they really knew the answers to most things (even if they didn't). Instead, they seemed to want us to "understand" them. Well, we already had enough members in the Sad Souls Club, and anyhow it wasn't for grownups.

There was a sound behind us and the louvered door from the house to the terrace opened slightly. For a few seconds nothing more happened, and then suddenly Rosebud's blonde head popped out like a puppet's from behind a curtain on a miniature stage. Her face was perfectly made up, as always — rosy-pink satin mouth, midnight-blue satin eyelids, long satiny dark eyelashes (were they false, too?). She was wearing a white, two-piece bathing suit. For the first time I noticed that she was a little thick in the waist and her thighs were really hefty. But she was a luscious, even, coppery-rose tan all over, and naturally her skin looked great against the white.

"D-a-a-r-r-r-lings," she cried, blowing me a smiling kiss, "I feel so guilty. Tess is doing such beautiful things in the kitchen with avocados and shrimps and mayonnaise and I-don't-know-what. I'm sure I should be helping her instead of luxuriating out here in the pool. But, oh, that water does look so wonderful." She turned to me. "Why don't you come in with me, Tina, d-a-a-r-r-r-ling? And you too, David?"

"Because we're both lazy," Pop said, smiling indulgently at Rosebud. "Well, not Tina, really. She's been writing a letter."

"What pretty stationery!" Rosebud exclaimed, sidling up to my chair and openly reading the name and address on the envelope over my shoulder.

I didn't say anything.

"Go on in and enjoy your swim," Pop advised Rosebud. "I'm going to go and have a shower myself." He stood up and we both watched Rosebud dive into the pool. She was a strong swimmer, not very graceful but terribly powerful. You felt she could have swum the English Channel in a single afternoon.

"She's really something, isn't she?" Pop commented admiringly.

I glanced up at him, squinting while attempting to shade my eyes with one arm. "Why is she called Rosebud, anyway?" I asked. "Is that a Hungarian name or what?"

"I don't know," Pop said. Then he spun around, giving the head of the racket a single, brisk tap against his palm. "You can ask her all about that and anything else you want to know at lunch. See you then." And he vanished into the house.

A few minutes later Nellie, who came in days to do the cleaning, called out that Nana Tess wanted me to set the table on the terrace for lunch. And promptly at one o'clock we all sat down to eat, including Arthur who was still red and hot-looking from a morning of bicycle riding.

Rosebud was in great spirits and Pop seemed artificially gay. Nana Tess kept jumping up from the table a lot, going back and forth to the kitchen for this and that. Finally, she brought out the desserts on a big tray, set it down with a loud clatter, and said, "For heaven's sake, David, are you or aren't you?"

Pop laughed and he seemed to blush under his tan, while Rosebud made big eyes and smiled at everyone. I still hadn't gotten around to asking her about her name.

"Is he or isn't he *what?*" Arthur asked. "What's up? Are we having some sort of surprise?" He turned to Nana Tess. "Why'd you keep telling me to be sure to be back at quarter to one for lunch today? You told me over and over again. What is it, a special occasion?"

Rosebud leaned forward and blew Arthur a kiss. She had changed into a pale yellow dress with a low frilly neckline. "Oh, Arthur, you *are* a d-a-a-r-r-r-ling," she gushed. "You've guessed."

"No, I haven't," he said, frowning. "Guessed what? I still don't know." He turned to me with a baffled look. "Does anybody?"

"Search me," I shrugged, rolling my eyes up toward the heavens. I was still feeling annoyed about no one's telling me the divorce was final. Not that it mattered, I suppose, since Mom and Pop were never getting together again.

Nana Tess handed round the desserts, some kind of pudding or custard with raspberry sauce on it, and sat down firmly at the table. "Well, children," she said, in a pebbly, low-pitched voice that sounded both serious and expectant, "since poor David seems too shy to come out with it, and I guess Rosebud feels it wouldn't be her place to tell you, *I* might as well break the news. Your father and Rosebud are engaged to be married! Now what do you think about that?"

I pushed back my chair, which made a horrible scraping noise on the flagstones, and began twitching my nose ferociously. Pop and Rosebud just sat there beaming, waiting, I suppose, to be congratulated. But my throat was as dry as my nostrils. I couldn't say a thing.

Only Arthur spoke. Always practical, he wanted to know, "When?"

Rosebud turned to Pop coyly. "September, David?" If they hadn't agreed on a date before, they seemed to be agreeing on one now.

I cleared my throat. "Uh . . . I always meant to ask you . . ." I said to Rosebud, "about your name. Is that a Hungarian name? Rosebud?"

"Yes," she answered, looking very pleased, as though I'd just asked her the most delightful question in the world. "But Rosebud itself is, of course, not a Hungarian word; it is an English translation of 'baby Rose' or 'tiny little Rose,' the name I was called when I was very small. Rose, or Rosa, is, however, my true Hungarian name."

"So why are you still called Rosebud?" Arthur inquired. "You're not tiny now."

Rosebud's smile faded slightly. "No, of course not," she said flirtatiously. "I'm a big girl now. But that is still my name." And she dug vigorously into her dessert, making it very clear that the conversation was closed.

Nana Tess said pointedly, "I haven't heard anybody around this table say 'Congratulations,' but *I* will right now. And the best of luck to both of you!"

Arthur and I mumbled, "Congratulations," and Pop and Rosebud dipped their heads in acknowledgment like a fairy prince and princess, with all their courtiers and subjects kneeling down around them.

"Now that's done with," said Nana Tess, pushing her empty dessert plate away, "I can tell you children *my* news."

Arthur stopped eating, his mouth full and his spoon poised in midair, dribbling pudding. "Don't tell me *you're* getting married, *too*," he muttered, half-wearily and half-disgustedly.

Nana Tess pushed Arthur's arm and spoon down toward his dessert dish so the pudding wouldn't drip on the table or into his lap. "Heaven forbid," she laughed hoarsely. "Widow is my middle name by now. No, something even better." She glanced at Pop and Rosebud. "For me, that is. I'm going to Europe, to Greece, and the Greek Islands. And it's on very short notice because I'm filling in for Harriet Frimble, who broke her ankle playing golf the other day. In fact, I'm leaving in exactly one week."

"What about us?" Arthur exclaimed, pushing out his lower lip. "*They're* getting married," he pointed an accusing finger at Pop and Rosebud as though they were a pair of deserters, "and *you're* going away. What are *we* supposed to do?"

"Yes," I muttered, my fury mounting at

all these grownups with their 'surprises.' "What are we supposed to do?"

"Well, that's just it," Nana Tess said, "if you'll let me finish. David — your dad — and I thought it might be a good idea for you two to go and stay with your — with Midge for a while. It would be a nice chance for you two to get reacquainted with her. And, of course, it would only be for three weeks. Until I return from my trip. You'd be back here again before school opens."

I got to my feet so suddenly the chair nearly fell over. "No thanks," I said flatly. This time no amount of twitching was going to prevent my nose from closing up on me. My nostrils would become sealed together, no matter what. Permanently. Forever.

"Tina, sit down," Nana Tess commanded. "Let's talk about this sensibly. Why don't you want to go there?"

Arthur answered for me. "She doesn't want to go there because it's dirty and it's old and it's cruddy and it smells bad and it's polluted. There isn't anything to do or anyone to be with, and there's no place to ride a bike. There *is* this pretty dog, though. His name's Wart. And there's this fella that cooks the food. He makes the greatest — "

My mind pounced. "That's right!" I said. I

had to find some really good reason for our not going to stay at Midge's. "There's this man who lives in the apartment with her. I don't know who he is or what he's doing there. All I know is his name's Peter and he does all the shopping and cooking for her. And I don't think Mom's rich enough to hire a cook . . ."

Pop had gotten up and come around to my side of the table. He put an arm around my shoulders and said soothingly, "Calm down, Tina. It's okay. We know all about it. I met Peter. And I saw the apartment, too. It's not nearly as bad as you two are making out. Do you think Nana Tess or I would even suggest such a thing if . . ."

Arthur jumped up. He had finally finished his pudding, spooning up the very last of it from the bottom of the dish. "But I still don't see why we couldn't stay here while Nana Tess is away, and then I could still ride my bike and play with the kids like always." He turned to Rosebud. "And why couldn't you come and take care of us if you're going to be — going to be our mother, sort of, anyway?"

Rosebud's laughter tinkled out like too many different-sounding bells at once. "Arthur, d-a-a-r-r-r-ling! Thank you for the compliment." (What compliment?) "But I am afraid it is too soon for me to be a mother. I'm not even a bride yet. I like you both so much, of course. But give me a chance, won't you?"

Arthur was already turning away. No use trying in that direction.

"But," Rosebud wasn't finished, "the other situation, for you and Tina to go to your real mother for a while, well, don't you see that is a fine idea." Rosebud's eyes met mine where I stood with Pop's arm still around my shoulders. "And you, Tina, you mustn't worry about your mother and Peter, d-a-a-r-r-r-ling, for to give you the whole truth, they are *married*. So there. Now, you see, everything is fine."

I could feel Pop start. "Rosebud!" he said in alarm. "*We* weren't supposed to tell them. *She* was."

"But now it's come up, d-a-a-r-r-r-ling," she answered him sweetly, innocently lifting both hands, palms up. "So, of course, we had to. Anyhow, they would soon have been told."

Pop didn't say another word. But I couldn't help feeling he agreed with Rosebud.

"Well," Arthur said, scratching his head, "now I'm *all* mixed up because of all these different mothers and fathers. To tell you the truth, I think Peter is an awful sissy. I never heard of a father spending all his time in the kitchen and not going to any office or anything. But he makes terrific hot fudge sauce. The best! And he told me he has this super recipe for black walnut fudge. So, I'm willing to go, I guess. As long as it's only going to be for three weeks. . . ."

My fingers clutched the back of the chair that I was still standing behind. "Only because you're a disgusting little glutton!" I screamed at him. "Go, if you want to. Go ahead and *drown* yourself in hot fudge sauce. I hope you do. But *I'm* not going. I'm sick and tired of being pushed around for everybody else's convenience and never being told anything. Everybody wants to be understood, but nobody wants to understand *me!* I have my friends here and my club here and this is where I'm staying. You're not going to budge me. None of you!" And I ducked out from under Pop's arm and headed for the house.

Nana Tess had been slowly thumping with her fingers on the edge of the table, her lips pursed and her sharp eyes fixed on me in a silent, exasperated stare. But Rosebud called out after me. "Tina, you're acting like a very selfish child. I'm sure you're going to be very sorry for this and then you will change your mind and apologize."

I turned and came back a few steps, closer to where Rosebud sat. There was a bee, a honeybee, that I had been watching with fascination for some time, nearly drowning in the remains of the raspberry sauce in Rosebud's dessert dish. Now it suddenly flew up out of the sauce and began to buzz cozily around one of the yellow ruffles at Rosebud's chest.

"There's a bee on your chest, Rosebud," I remarked quite calmly.

She jumped up with a start and began swatting at the yellow ruffles with both hands while Pop, who was back at her side, waved a napkin in front of her wildly.

"You're both doing exactly the wrong thing," I declared. "Anyhow, Rosebud, you're wearing yellow, so he'll probably sting you no matter what you do. They almost always sting people who are wearing yellow!"

My anger had flared up again. In fact, I was furious, even more furious than Rosebud's bee. Nose twitching, I turned and ran off to my room.

5

Ina and I were sitting up in Ina's room and talking. Two weeks had passed since the day of the lunch with Rosebud and all the "announcements." Nana Tess had departed for Greece a week ago, and Arthur had gone to stay with Mom and Peter in the city. Ina and I were whispering because it was 1:45 in the morning, a Friday night, and downstairs in the living room we could hear Mrs. Harris, the baby-sitter, gently snoring.

As you can imagine, Ina's mother wasn't hiring any more teen-age baby-sitters even though it was like locking the barn after the horse (in this case, Ina's father) had been stolen. Mrs. Harris was around sixty, with gray-brown hair and musty breath. Of course, Ina and I could easily have baby-sat for Ina's twin sisters, aged eight, instead of being baby-sat *for* by the snoring Mrs. Harris. But Mrs. Philips, Ina's mother, said she was nervous enough these days without taking any unnecessary risks. And I guess having me stay with them was an added responsibility. I wasn't at Ina's all the time, of course, because Nellie still came to Nana Tess's each day to keep things tidy, and Pop was there most evenings. But usually I did spend nights and weekends at Ina's. So I'd managed to avoid having to go and stay at Midge's, and I was feeling pretty smug about that.

"I'm starving," Ina had said from the other bed at about one o'clock, "and I can't sleep. In fact, I have this terrible insomnia." So we'd both gone downstairs and brought up peanut-butter-and-marshmallow-fluff sandwiches, cookies, pretzels, and a quart carton of chocolate milk. "This'll do it," Ina said, tearing into the first sandwich. "We'll sleep like babies."

Ina's reducing diet, if she'd ever had one, was going to the devil. But I'd given up caring, at least for the time being. She said she was too jittery to think about dieting now that her mother was dating so much and always with the same man.

"Suppose she marries this Walter P. Dribble," Ina moaned, her lips lathered with marshmallow fluff.

"Drabble," I corrected. "I thought you told me his name was Drabble."

"Drabble, Dribble, Drivel, what's the difference? He's really nothing but an old fogey dressed up in expensive sports clothes, with artificial tanning makeup on his face and a rinse to make his hair look silvery instead of dishwater gray. Can't she see that?"

"Well, maybe it doesn't matter to her. Maybe she feels safer with him. And didn't you tell me he was rich, that he was in the real estate business or something?"

Ina gulped some milk. "So what? I never heard anybody worry about money as much as she does. She's always afraid my father'll stop sending the money and only keep on sending the grapefruit. Mortgage, mortgage, mortgage — that's her favorite subject. How will she manage to keep paying the mortgage on the house? Meanwhile, I don't see anybody starving around here. Do you?"

"No," I said, looking pointedly across the bed at Ina. "Hardly."

"And," Ina went on, unperturbed, reaching for a pecan-crunch butter cookie, "there are young, handsome men around who have some money, too. Look at your fa — "

From sitting cross-legged at the foot of the bed, Ina suddenly scrambled onto her hands and knees, nearly dumping the whole midnight lunch. "Hey! What *about* your father? Hey, listen to this. What an idea I've got! Your father and my mother. Now why didn't I ever think of that before? That way we could get rid of Rosebud and Mr. Drivel both at once. And we could all live together, in one house, with no money worries, as one family . . ."

"They've already met, Ina."

"And you and I would be sisters. . . ."

"Ina," I reminded her, "they've met. Remember? In fact, they meet every time Pop brings me here to sleep over because he's going out on a date with Rosebud for the evening. And they've never even noticed one another except to say, 'Here's Tina,' and 'Thank you,' and 'No trouble,' and 'I'll pick her up in the morning,' and so on. It won't work, Ina. Forget it. He's hooked on Rosebud."

Ina sat back, thinking. How could I possibly tell her that I had already heard Rosebud discussing Mrs. Philips' visit to the tennis courts at the club and calling her "a very dull pudding of a woman with an abominable serve," to which Pop had readily agreed?

Just then a car drove up outside, its expensive engine soft and muffled, and we both padded over to Ina's window, which overlooked the front entrance of the house. Mr. Drabble got out, went around to the passenger's side, opened the door for Mrs. Philips, and escorted her to the front door, which we soon heard opening.

Mr. Drabble had a very deep voice that seemed to give off heavy vibrations but no clearly understood words. Mrs. Philips was speaking in soft murmurs.

"Ugh," Ina said, clapping her hands over her ears and rushing to close the door of her room and block out any further sounds from the downstairs hall. They were probably going to wake up Mrs. Harris now so Mr. Drabble could drive her home.

"I'm nauseous," Ina said, coming back to the bed with her hands over her stomach. "I need a pretzel. Did you know that dry things with salt on them are very good for a nauseous stomach?"

"I don't know what you're carrying on about," I said, preparing to go back to my own bed and to sleep. "I've got your very same problem, only double. How would you like your mother married to a man who makes fudge and your father engaged to a blonde phony who calls everybody d-a-a-r-r-r-ling?"

"No problem at all," Ina said soberly. "I'd kill myself."

The next day was Saturday, and the Sad Souls Club was scheduled to meet at Amy's house at two o'clock. On the Saturday before, the club had met at Ina's. It had been the first meeting with Karla present and I was surprised at how quiet she had been. Most of the time she had just sat and listened, and once or twice she giggled, with her hands over her mouth, when Ina was reporting (under Beauty Tips) from an article she had read in a magazine about wearing yellow eye shadow in summer because it gave you "that warm sun-drenched look." Karla didn't even have anything to say when Ina modeled the yellow eye shadow, and everyone was disappointed and agreed it made her look like she had yellow jaundice, around the eyes anyway. She only giggled some more. Of course, Karla hadn't been assigned any reports of her own to give yet, because it was only her first week in the club. But she wasn't going to get away with that at this meeting.

By two-fifteen, Amy, Ina, and I were holed up in the upstairs TV room in Amy's house. Karla wasn't there yet. She had told Amy she had a dentist's appointment around twelve-thirty and to start without her if she was late. So we did.

Under Old Business, we took up Cokie's answer to my letter. Cokie agreed to the club name I'd suggested: Cokie the Curvature, "but only because all the others are perfectly terrible, too, and because they must and always will remain deep, dark secrets." Cokie also wrote that she had met a boy at camp who seemed to like her quite a bit but "as you would expect, he has teeth braces, eyeglasses, and acne. All the cute ones are taken by the popular girls. Like always."

Amy sighed, as if from long experience. "Isn't that always the way it is? But I suppose she needs to stick to him. Otherwise, it's just awful at dances and weenie roasts when everybody pairs off and you're left over — along with the ugliest or fattest girl in your bunk." She turned with a jolt to Ina, her hand clapped over her mouth. "Oops, sorry. I didn't mean anything personal, you understand."

"It's perfectly all right," Ina said loftily. Anyhow, I *am* losing weight. I took off fourteen ounces this week."

"Fourteen ounces!" I exclaimed. "That's not even a pound."

Ina chose to ignore me. "I've got a suggestion under Beauty Tips for Amy," she said. So we went on to Regular Business. "It's about these new velvet fingernails. They're going to be very big for fall."

Amy, who bit her nails, squinted. "What are *they*?"

"They're fake, but very gorgeous. Come in all colors, like midnight black, deep purple, burgundy red. Very furry and soft. Waterproof. You paste them on. Now could you bite through velvet? Wouldn't that just make you want to scream?"

"No," Amy said coolly. "It wouldn't make me want to scream at all. I'd bite."

"Oh, you're hopeless," Ina blubbered, waving a hand disgustedly at Amy.

"Where's Karla, anyway?" I asked impatiently, looking at my watch. It was now twenty-five minutes to three. "She was supposed to report on Hobbies and Recreation. She said she was going to have some good party ideas. If she was so anxious to join the SSSC, why doesn't she show up at meetings?"

Amy got up and glanced out the window from which she could see part of the garden behind Karla's house, next door. The swimming pool still didn't have any water in it. "Don't worry," she said. "She'll be here. Meanwhile, I'll do my report on scents. I wandered around in Grover's Drugs this morning and picked up some body-oil samples."

"Oh, good!" Ina said eagerly. "Where are they?"

Amy came over to where Ina and I were sitting on the studio couch side by side. "Close your eyes," she commanded, "so all your other senses will be blocked out."

Ina and I sat there sniffing with our eyes shut. I leaned forward, sniffing harder, because I still didn't smell anything special, and bumped my chin into something medium-soft and fleshy. My eyes flew open. "What's that! What is it?"

"My arm, you dopes," Amy said. "The samples. Sniff! They're on my arm. You didn't think I was going to bring whole bottles of the stuff, did you? They're expensive."

Ina and I sniffed some more, our nostrils practically resting on Amy's extended right arm. "You must have the wrong arm," I said. "This one smells . . . well, sour if you must know. Like rotten apples."

"That's it!" Amy said triumphantly. "The name of the scent. It's called Sour Apples Body Oil — 'natural, fresh, tangy, nippy, and tart.' Do you like it?"

"No," I said. "It's awful." Ina nodded in agreement.

"Well, that's out then," Amy said, not caring much. "Try this one." She put her right arm behind her back and lifted her left arm, moving it slowly until it came to rest under our noses. "You should close your eyes, though." Ina closed her eyes and inhaled deeply.

"Oh, much nicer," Ina said, breathing even harder. "It's exactly like rice pudding. The creamy kind."

"I agree," I said, even though I'd kept my eyes open this time. "Something like that. Only who wants to smell like rice pudding? Suppose you're going out with a boy and he really hates rice pudding?"

"I still like it," Ina said dreamily. "What's it called? Rice Pudding Body Oil?"

"Oh, you," I said. "You like anything that reminds you of food."

"It isn't *called* Rice Pudding," Amy said, scratching her head and unsettling her latest gamin haircut. "It's something like Cinnamon-Vanilla or Vanilla-Cinnamon, or maybe its called Spicy Vanilla. Or maybe Vanilla Spice. I'm not really too sure. I forgot to write it down. They have it at Grover's though. It's on the counter right next to Sour Apples. Or maybe the name of that one was really Green Apples."

"Never mind," I said, forgiving Amy for once for her terrible memory. "Almost nobody likes sour apples and, from what I've heard, most boys don't like cinnamon *or* vanilla. I once knew a girl who wrote to a boy on writing paper that she kept in a drawer with cinnamon sachet. She made the sachet herself from her mother's cooking spices. When the letter came, the boy was so embarrassed by the smell he threw it away as soon as he read it and never answered it."

"That would never happen to me," Ina murmured, dipping her head for still another sniff of Amy's arm.

"Of course not," I retorted. "Who would you write to in the first place?"

As soon as I said it, I was sorry. But I

was getting short-tempered because I was feeling impatient and annoyed, not at Ina but at Karla. "Where is she anyway?" I fumed. It was now after three P.M.

"Where's who?" Amy wanted to know, pointy nose lifted and glasses glinting.

"Well, Karla, of course."

Amy shrugged.

"I just hope she's not out shoplifting," I said sternly. "She hasn't been doing anything like that, has she?"

Amy looked indignant. "Of course not. She doesn't want to get thrown out of the club, does she?"

"Maybe she's already quit us. Maybe she took something from Grover's or the five-and-dime, so she disqualified herself and was too ashamed to show up at the meeting."

"Oh, Tina!" Ina said. "Maybe she's still at the dentist's, in just horrible pain. Think of it. She might not be able to eat for days."

"All right," I said firmly. "The meeting ends at four. If she's not here by three-thirty, she's marked absent and that's that. Three absences as a probationary member and she's out automatically. Meanwhile, I could give my report on transparent makeup and fruit-flavored lip glosses. Should I?"

I was actually wearing the makeup and

so far nobody had noticed. Was that a good sign or a bad sign? It was a "tissue thin" liquid that came in a little bottle and was supposed to give your skin "that glowing, natural look."

Amy and Ina smeared some on their faces, too. Then we tried on the lip glosses — tangerine, peach, and strawberry. They tasted pretty good when you licked your lips. I suppose the idea was to find a flavor that a boy would like if he kissed you. What boy though? When? Would it ever happen and what would it feel like if it did? And would we like it or hate it?

Ina's lip gloss got licked off in no time at all, of course, and Amy said she'd go downstairs and get the refreshments. I picked up a large hand mirror that Amy had brought from her mother's bedroom, and I went to the window where the light was better to decide about this transparent makeup. Did it or didn't it give me a "glow"? I just wasn't sure. The lip gloss was nice, though. I had put the strawberry on my upper lip and the tangerine on my lower.

I was still studying the two pastel shades of lip gloss when suddenly a flash of something bright raspberry-pink caught my eye. The color wasn't reflected in the mirror; it seemed to be somewhere alongside it. I moved the mirror away from my face and looked directly out through the window. There, down in Karla's garden, only just visible between a large, leafy tree and the side of the house, was the moving figure of a girl. The figure was walking a bicycle, had shining auburn hair, and was dressed in jeans and a raspberry-pink shirt. Beside it there was another figure, just hopping off a bicycle. It was tall, taller than Karla, was male, had dark golden hair with darker streaks in it, and parted lips that showed unmistakable toothpaste-ad teeth.

I stood there transfixed. It must have been a whole minute before I gasped, "Ina!" She was busy nibbling at the plate of cookies Amy had brought up before going back downstairs for the lemonade.

"What?" Ina panted, jumping up and coming to my side at once. Something in my voice must have told her this was a serious situation.

The two figures down in the garden were sticking close to the side of the house, and if they were talking to one another, we couldn't hear them, especially with the window closed because the air-conditioning was on. Ina's hands flew to her hips. "Well, I like that," she said, puffing with exasperation. "What's she doing with *him*, anyway? How'd she even meet him? She only just moved into the neighborhood."

Amy came into the room, muttering something about having spilled part of the lemonade on the stairs.

"Never mind about that," Ina hissed, as though Karla Hunt and Tiger Rawson down below in the garden could hear her. "Come on over here to the window this minute and take a look. Just take a look at *that*." She nearly poked a finger through the glass pane.

Amy put down the lemonade, came over to the window, and peered out. "Oh, there she is," she exclaimed, sounding pleased and not particularly surprised. "See, I told you she'd show up. Here, help me lift the window. I'll call out to her and tell her we're up here. She's just in time for the lemonade."

"No," I said, holding on to my place of command in the center of the window frame. "I don't want her to know we've seen her. Don't you see who she's with? What's she doing with him if she's supposed to be here with us? I'd like to find out if she's going to come to this meeting on her own or not."

But it was too late. Amy had already unfastened the window lock, and the next moment she raised the window so eagerly that it flew wide open. The noise was like the sharp snap of a window shade on a busted roller, and down in Karla's garden the two heads shot upward with a start.

Karla immediately saw me standing in the open window with Ina and Amy on either side. For an instant she appeared stunned, and then she started jumping up and down and waving both hands like a cheerleader.

"Hi Tina, Amy, Ina! Hi!" She was smiling broadly. "Is the meeting still on? Am I awfully late? Hang on. I'll be up there in a jiffy."

Tiger, who had come up close behind her, stood there grinning and mumbled something to her. She turned to listen to him for a moment and then turned back to us. "There's somebody here with me — Tiger Rawson. He says he knows you, Tina. Do you know him?"

"I know him, all right." I was staring down angrily at the two of them, my throat very dry and my nose twitching uncontrollably. "But I wouldn't say we were friends," I managed to add.

Tiger stepped forward, his eyes dancing, and the wicked grin still on his lips. "Yep, there she is. That's her, all right. The little lady, half-human and half-bunny, who twitches her nose like a rabbit." He was clearly showing off for Karla, who was giggling with make-believe embarrassment, both hands covering her mouth.

Tiger stuck his thumbs beneath his armpits like a carnival barker, planted his legs farther apart, and called out, even louder, "So step right up, everybody, step up and see the world's tallest lady-rabbit, Miss Tina Carstairs! The girl with the fastest-twitching nose on earth. Yessirree, the famous, the unbeatable, the world-renowned TINA C., THE TEEN-AGE TWITCH!"

Karla's eyes opened wide and her hands flew away from her mouth. She wasn't laughing anymore. She gaped up at my rigid, icy face, with the nose I suppose still twitching, and shrieked, "I didn't tell him. I swear to you, all of you — Tina, Ina, Amy — I never told him a single one of our secret club names. I never did! I swear it! It's the truth. I honestly hope you believe me."

"It doesn't matter," I screamed back at her, before either of the others could speak. "It's *your* fault. It's *still* your fault. And I'm never going to forgive you for it. Never!"

I reached up, gave the window one ferocious tug, and slammed it shut.

6

Sunday. It was late morning and I was sitting on the floor in Arthur's room and playing jacks because the vinyl flooring was harder in there and made the ball bounce better.

The house was completely empty and, so far as I knew, nobody else knew I was there. I'd come home directly after slamming the window on Karla and Tiger, even running breathlessly into Karla on the front steps of Amy's house as I was dashing out and she was rushing in, full of explanations and apologies. But, of course, I'd refused to talk to her. And Tiger, naturally, had already vanished, having sped away on his bike.

At Nana Tess's house, I'd let myself in with the key. Nellie was already gone and Pop's car wasn't in the driveway. I took a cold supper of cream cheese and jelly sandwiches from the refrigerator, watched TV until very late, and finally went to bed. If Pop came home to sleep during the night, *I* didn't know it, and *he* probably never looked in my room, so he didn't know *I* was there.

What was I going to do now? There were still two weeks to go before Nana Tess came back from Greece and Arthur came back from Midge and Peter's. I could go back to staying part-time at Ina's, but not until she and Amy agreed that Karla should be kicked out of the club. Otherwise, there just wasn't going to be any more SSSC.

A car pulled up outside the house and the doorbell rang. I went downstairs and looked out carefully to see who it was before answering the door. It was Mrs. Philips and Ina. Mrs. Philips was wearing tight aquamarine pants and a matching, tight, low-cut blouse with lots of long glittery strands of jewelry around her neck. She looked tired and sleepy and had dark rings under her eyes. She poked her head inside as soon as I opened the door and looked around quickly.

"Am I glad you're here! I was sure you were supposed to sleep over at our house last night. But I had so much on my mind. There was this realty association dinner-dance." Mrs. Philips ran one hand through the disarranged curls of her short, strawberry-blonde hair. "I didn't get home until a quarter to five this morning. I'm utterly dead, I can tell you."

Mr. Drabble again, no doubt. I looked meaningfully at Ina, who was acting strangely quiet.

"Now," Mrs. P. went on, "Ina tells me you had to leave the club meeting early yesterday afternoon and she has a lot to tell you about what happened afterward. So, suppose I leave her here and you can both walk back to our house for lunch later on if you like."

I nodded, while Ina stepped into the living room and Mrs. Phillips turned to leave. "By the way," Mrs. Philips said, with a sudden note of alarm in her voice, "you didn't spend the night here alone, did you?"

"No," I said quickly. "Of course not." Actually, I couldn't be sure whether this was the truth or not. Pop *might* have been home.

"And where's your father now?" she asked, a little more relaxed.

"Oh, he's at the club playing tennis." Again there was a pretty good chance this was the truth.

"But he'll be back shortly, I suppose."

"Oh, sure," I said confidently.

Mrs. Philips sighed. "Motherless children, fatherless children . . . it's all so sad. So very sad. Deserting those we once loved." Her voice drifted off.

I closed the door behind her and Ina shrugged.

"So?" she said.

"So?" I repeated.

For the first time I could remember, I didn't feel at ease with Ina. Something seemed wrong. "Why don't we go out and sit by the pool?" I suggested. I didn't want her to come upstairs and find out I'd been sitting on the floor in Arthur's room all morning, playing jacks.

We both went through the dining room doors out onto the pool terrace and plunked down into chairs. I stared at her. Her face was dull, expressionless.

"What's with you, anyway? You're acting awfully funny."

"Nothing's with me," she said. "You're the one who's been acting funny."

"I hope you don't call walking out on Karla 'acting funny,'" I replied. "Admit it. You were as angry as I was when you saw them down in the garden. Why was she hanging out with him when she should have been at the meeting? And it *was* her fault he called me — that name — again. Couldn't you see she was playing up to him and he was trying to make a big impression on her? And making fun of *me* to do it, using me. Oh, the whole thing's disgusting! I don't even want to talk about it." I waved an arm in angry dismissal.

Ina glanced toward the pool. She seemed to be avoiding my eyes. "Well, I know," she said slowly. "I was angry, too. At first."

"What do you mean, 'at first'?" I pounced. "Oh, I suppose she came skipping in all breathless and sorry and told you two some wild story about why she was late, and you both forgave her because she's so sweet and pretty and her hair always bounces back into place so beautifully...."

"It was true," Ina interrupted. "She did go to the dentist. And he had some kind of an emergency with another patient and she had to wait a long time, and then she had to have X rays taken."

"And who should she be formally introduced to at the dentist's office but Tiger Rawson because the dentist keeps him around to show off his toothpaste-commercial teeth, and Tiger said, 'Oh, please, Miss Hunt, you are so gloriously beautiful and have such cute teeth yourself, do allow me to accompany you home, side by side on our stalwart bicycles.'"

"No," Ina said defensively. "You're just being sarcastic. That's not the way it happened at all."

"Oh, really," I said, even more sarcastically. "Then do tell me how it really happened. According, of course, to someone who is already a known shoplifter and a liar."

"Well," Ina said, ignoring my remark and intent on telling Karla's story, "she had an errand she had promised to do for her brother who's away on a camping trip for two weeks. Did you know Karla has an older brother who's fourteen-and-a-half?"

"No. What's that got to do with it?"

"Well," Ina went on soberly, "he — her brother, that is — signed up for a paper route right after they moved in, and Tiger is in charge of distribution for the whole district.

So, after the dentist, she went over to Tiger's house, because she promised her brother she would, to ask him if she could take over the route for her brother until he gets back so he won't lose it. And Tiger said yes. Isn't that great? And that's how come he rode back with her. Because she had to fill in some papers and he had to sign them."

"Oh, wow!" I said, bursting with disbelief. "That's quite a story."

But Ina ignored that, too, and went on blithely, getting more and more excited. "But wait. You didn't hear the best part. Karla is going to have a pool party at her house next Friday night — with colored lights, a barbecue, dancing, and everything. We're all invited — you, me, Amy. And there'll be boys. Plenty of boys."

"Tiger?"

"Of course. And he promised to bring along about six friends."

I shot to my feet. "Ina, you're an idiot! Why didn't we call you Ina the Idiot instead of Ina the Insomniac?"

Ina looked up at me, more stricken than insulted.

"Why? What's wrong? Look, Tina, wait a minute. We have to talk about this. I know how you feel about Tiger. But he won't be the only one there. There'll be lots of other boys. And anyhow he was only teasing you. Karla says it probably means he likes you. And she absolutely promised that she would get him to promise not to call you that anymore. I knew you wouldn't come to the party otherwise. I told her that. And Karla really likes you, Teen. She felt awful when you wouldn't talk to her yesterday when you were leaving Amy's house."

I stared at her in horror.

"Tina, why are you looking at me that way? I'm only trying to fix everything up so we can all be friends. And the party sounds like a terrific idea. It'll give us a head start for junior high. You know, that's when it really all begins, and how else would we ever get any practice? Karla says the trouble with the Sad Souls Club is it's all talk and no action. She says just sitting around and trying on makeup and talking about boy and family problems and hobbies and recreation isn't enough. We have to get out and *do* it. That's the only way we'll ever develop our personalities. I honestly think we could learn a lot from her. And which one of *us* knows enough boys to invite for a really good get-together? Don't you see what I mean?"

I was standing over at the edge of the pool

watching a large, lacy-patterned, pale-yellow butterfly that had alighted on the surface of the water, gotten too wet, and was probably going to drown. Ina was still sitting in the chair, but leaning forward now, her voice full of urging.

I turned around. "No, I don't see what you mean. Do you actually think you're going to have a good time at that party? Do you think you're going to lose twenty pounds and get to look as good as Karla by next Friday? Can't you see she's using you? You and Amy. Only not me, because I'm not going to her party. She's the kind who'll climb on everybody's back to get where she wants to be, and once she's up at the top she's going to kick away all the people who helped get her there. And as for Tiger, forget it. He's hers. Until she finds somebody she likes even better. I know you've got a crush on him, so I'm just warning you for your own good."

Ina hurled herself up out of the chair.

"Why, Tina," she protested, "I have not. How can you say a thing like that?"

"Oh, quit it, Ina," I snapped. "You have, too. It was you who called out to him that day in the playground when he wanted Arthur to throw him the basketball: 'Why don't you come over here and get it?'" I mimicked Ina's wheedling, flirtatious tone. "And that was when he came over and called *me* that — that name. It never would have happened if you hadn't started with him."

"Oh," Ina said, growing indignant. "I suppose I can't say what I want to whomever I please. I suppose now you're blaming me for all your troubles. Just like you're blaming Karla for yesterday. Well, did it ever occur to you, Tina, that the reason Tiger called you a twitch is because you are one? Even now you're twitching your nose like crazy. He was right. I'm supposed to be your friend, so I'm telling it to you straight, Tina. It's the truth you can't stand!"

"No," I flared. "You're wrong. It's lies I can't stand. Karla's lies and your lies . . . and everybody's lies."

"*My* lies! I never lied to you."

"Maybe you did and maybe you didn't. But you sure are lying to yourself. All the time. Why don't you face the truth about how overweight you are and how you keep on eating all the time, always feeding yourself excuses. I tried to help you. I practically started the Sad Souls Club to help you — and Amy and Cokie and myself, too, of course. I tried to find all kinds of good reducing diets for you. But you never listened.

And now you've busted up the club and you want to do things Karla's way. Okay, do it. Go to her party. Go! And I hope the whole bunch of you fall in the empty pool. It'll serve you right!"

Ina, who had already marched herself halfway through the garden to the driveway that led out to the street, stopped and turned around. "Oh, by the way," she taunted, "I forgot to tell you the pool is going to be cleaned out and filled up for the party. There's going to be swimming, too."

"That's even better," I called out after her, visualizing fat Ina in her bathing suit alongside Karla in her bikini. "I hope you make a real big splash with Tiger," I added nastily.

"Thank you," Ina said mockingly. "If you change your mind about coming to the party, don't bother to phone. It's already too late."

"Don't worry," I snarled. "You'll never hear from me!"

I was going to add something else, but Ina was already too far away to hear me, so instead I muttered the words under my breath: "And may your mother *definitely* decide to marry Mr. Drabble!"

It was going to be bread and jelly (the

cream cheese had run out) for Sunday lunch when a car zoomed into the driveway. This time it was Pop, in tennis shorts of course. So I'd been right about where he was and how soon he'd be coming home.

As he came toward me from the car, I watched behind him nervously for signs of Rosebud. Luckily, she didn't seem to be anywhere in sight. Pop wasn't walking as briskly as usual. He brightened up and smiled wanly, though, when he saw me.

"Sunflower! You here all alone?"

"Um hmmm," I said casually. "I thought I'd come over and hang around here today."

"Who brought you? You know I don't like you letting yourself into the house alone when Nellie or I aren't here."

"Oh, Mrs. Philips drove over this morning." That wasn't exactly the answer to Pop's question, but who could even begin to go into all the details?

Pop slumped into the chair where Ina had been sitting only a little while ago. "Well, I trounced them. But it was a tough tournament, let me tell you." Pop reminded me of Mrs. Philips, looking so 'morning-after' after the dinner-dance. Why were all these grown-up people knocking themselves out like this?

Pop rubbed his bronzed forehead, which

was covered with tiny droplets of perspiration. "So you decided to hang around here today, eh? I thought you liked it at Ina's."

I was walking catlike up and back along the edge of the pool, licking some of the jelly that had gotten on my fingers when I was opening the jar. "Well," I said, not looking at him, "that gets boring, too."

"Know what?" Pop said, beginning to sound more lively, "I'm kind of glad you're here. You and I haven't had much time together lately. And you look kind of mopey to me. I've got an idea. How about I take a shower and get into some clean duds, and you put on something pretty — a dress, maybe — and we go out and have ourselves a proper Sunday dinner."

"Where?" I asked suspiciously. I liked the idea. But I could already see Rosebud at the table making it a threesome.

"Anywhere you say. The club?"

"Uh-uh. Not the club. Someplace else. You did mean just the two of us, didn't you?"

"I did mean just the two of us. What about the Flying Dolphin? You could have a lobster, deep-fried clams, steamers, whatever."

My stomach gurgled, reminding me of how hungry I was. "Okay," I said, liking the idea better and better. "It sounds fine to me, and heaps better than a jelly sandwich. What should I wear? Never mind, I know. Let's go real soon, though, because I'm getting hungry enough to eat a deep-fried bear!"

It was a perfect day for the Dolphin, and since Pop knew the waiters and headwaiters everywhere, we got a table right on the water, where the small pleasure boats were moored at the Dolphin's private dock.

"Happy now, Sunflower?" Pop asked, when we'd ordered and the waiter had tied a big white plastic bib around my neck with a picture of a fiery red lobster in the center.

I nodded, and Pop looked out over the water and sighed. "This place has changed," he said. "Your mom and I used to come here when it was much smaller, more of a fisherman's hangout. You were just a tiny baby then."

"Did you call Mom some kind of flower in those days, too?" I asked.

Pop looked puzzled. "What do you mean?"

"Oh, you know, the way you call me Sunflower and you call Rosebud . . . well, Rosebud. Except, of course, I guess that really is her name. Or so she says."

Pop shook his head. "Nope, not that I can think of. Although, actually, I always thought she — Midge, that is — was very daisylike."

I put a tiny, crisp oyster cracker in my mouth and split it in two with my teeth. "Daisies? Never. To me, Mom seems more like a . . . like a pine tree, a tall straight one, very dark green."

Pop smiled, dipped his head in that 'anything-you-say' gesture, and took a sip of the tall, icy gin-and-tonic he'd ordered.

"You're not really upset about Rosebud, are you, Tina?" He looked very serious now.

"Rosebud's okay," I said, wishing my lobster would arrive so I could get busy eating it and not have to talk.

"But you do object to something about her, don't you? Tell me what it is. Come on, Sunflower, be honest with me for once."

"For once?" I said, looking up in surprise. "I'm honest. It's just that I'm never sure you really want to hear the truth about things."

Pop put his glass down and looked directly at me. I never realized before what really nice brown eyes he had. Level and clear.

"Okay," I said. "I'll tell you two absolutely honest things that are on my mind right this minute." Why was I suddenly coming out with all this? Maybe it was because of what Ina had said about my not wanting to face the truth. Well, she was dead wrong.

"Good!" Pop said. He took a long swig of his drink and set the glass down hard. "Shoot."

"Number one," I said, picking up my knife and fork, one in each hand, and holding them upright, fists on the table, "I don't like Rosebud. I think she's a phony. I'm sorry, but that's how I feel. And if you do marry her, I don't think I want to live with you. Ever. I think you just better send me off to boarding school, which might not be too bad an idea after all."

Pop didn't blink while I said all this. He didn't even look terribly upset. In fact, his expression never changed, so I just went on.

"And number two," I said, "number two . . ."

"Yes?" Pop leaned forward.

Suddenly the knife and fork fell from my hands and collapsed with a clatter on the table.

"Come on, Sunflower, you can tell me. What's number two?"

I lifted my eyes to try to look at Pop, and just as I expected, he was a big blur. He had about six heads, each one just a very little bit to the right of the one beside it.

"Number two," I managed to utter in a choked voice, "number two is that I'm . . . I'm having . . . a really awful summer. And I think . . . I think I'd like to go away someplace. Away from here." I was sobbing openly now. "Because I honestly . . . don't want to stay here anymore."

Pop looked really alarmed and pushed a large white handkerchief, very fine and fresh-smelling, across the table to me.

"Why, Sunflower, I had no idea it was this serious. You should have told me. I'll talk to Rosebud, I promise, and we'll put things off a while."

I shook my head furiously from side to side. "This isn't *about* Rosebud. I already told you about her. This is about me. I'm just not happy here anymore."

"But I thought you liked it. You've got your friends, your club. It was you who insisted on staying after Nana Tess and Arthur left."

"I know," I sniffed, most of my face buried in Pop's handkerchief, "but I don't like it now. Even Mom's place would be better."

Pop broke into a broad smile. "No problem, Sunflower. No problem at all. She'll be delighted to have you. Arthur, I'm sure, misses you. You can go any time. Any time at all. When do you want to go? Tomorrow?"

"Hot plate," a voice above me suddenly

cautioned. "Very hot plate," the waiter's voice repeated. "Promise you won't touch it, miss."

A huge oval platter of peppery-red lobster claws and snowy-white meat against a crimson shell was set down under my nose. I nodded while the waiter, napkin in hand, added a side dish of hot melted butter and a plate of sizzling French fried potatoes.

"It's a deal, then," Pop said jovially, as his own food — fried clams, shrimps, and scallops — was laid before him and he ordered an ice-cold beer to go with it. "We'll phone Midge tonight and tell her you're coming. Then you can pack a few things, and tomorrow morning you'll ride into town with me on the train." He lifted his fork. "See, any problem can be solved if we can just sit down and talk about it."

I attacked my lobster with a pair of claw-crackers and dug into the meat with the tiny, sharp-pronged fork. I wasn't exactly sure Pop was right. But going to Mom's *would* solve the problem of Ina, of Karla, of the wreckage of the SSSC, and of Karla's Friday-night party. Who knows, maybe history would even repeat itself? Maybe, like Mom, it was my turn to run away and never come back.

7

Arthur and Peter were waiting for us on Monday morning at Pennsylvania Station. It was odd seeing my "two fathers" together, as Pop handed over my small suitcase to Peter and they shook hands. While Pop was chatting with Arthur, hearing all about what he'd been doing this past week away from home, I was noticing that Peter was shorter than Pop, younger looking, and of course not nearly as handsome. It made me wonder what it was that Peter had and Pop didn't that had made Mom choose one over the other, aside from Peter's cooking of course. (And, in my eyes, *that* only made Peter seem pretty peculiar.)

Pop had to catch a subway train for downtown, where his office was, so after hugging Arthur good-by and kissing me, he turned to go. "So long, Sunflower. Have fun. I'll keep in touch with you by phone. And remember what we talked about yesterday. Honesty is the best policy."

Arthur turned to me. "What's that supposed to mean? Have you been telling a lot of lies lately?" He seemed pleased to see me, but he was also sticking pretty close to Peter. I noticed he was wearing a beaded Indian wristband.

"Don't be so nosy," I said, falling into step on the other side of Peter. "Where'd you get that thing you have on your arm?"

"It's made by real Indians," Arthur said, as if ready for a fight. "Peter took me to this museum way uptown. Everything you could want to see and know about American Indians is there. Headdresses, poison arrows, scary masks, even magic charms. See, this wristband has real moosehair woven into it. I got it in the museum shop. Everything they sell there is made by real Indians. Now, if you want to go to that museum today, we can. I don't mind going there again because I liked it a real lot. But if not, then there's other things we can do."

Peter laughed. "Right. Lots of things we can do. That's why I think we better sit down somewhere right now and find out what Tina would like to do today. I think she should have first pick. So suppose we go have some milk and doughnuts, and let's talk about it."

Peter, still carrying my suitcase, steered us to the coffee shop where we found a quiet corner at the end of the counter and ordered jelly doughnuts. Arthur, of course, decided to have a cream-filled doughnut covered with chocolate icing. What a glutton!

All this time I'd been wanting to ask about Mom, even though I knew what the answer would probably be. But I asked it anyway.

"Where's — uh — Midge this morning?"

Peter glanced at his watch. "Let's see, Monday, nine forty-five. Hard at work, I'd say, at her drawing board, almost getting ready to take her ten o'clock yogurt break."

It was what I had expected. I felt like commenting, "While you're out with the kiddies for the day," but of course I didn't.

What a topsy-turvy life they had. Even if it *was* supposed to be what Midge wanted. And as for Arthur, he didn't seem to notice anymore how mixed up it all was. Probably he was having too good a time to care.

But Peter must have been reading my thoughts. He pushed one of the jelly doughnuts, glistening with sugar crystals, toward me and said calmly, "But we'll see her this evening. In fact, I'm planning to cook a gala dinner in honor of your joining us."

Arthur bit into his doughnut and licked his lips, which were all squooshy with chocolate and custard. "So let's decide," he said earnestly, "what we're all gonna do today." He looked at Peter. "Should I give the suggestions or should you?"

I could see the two of them had really become teammates. It made me feel a little left out of things. Of course, there was still Mom. But she was so independent, and then she also had Peter.

"Do you want to go to the aquarium or the Statue of Liberty, or on a boatride or to the museum where the dinosaurs are, or . . ." Arthur wasn't really waiting for anybody else to make any suggestions. His cheeks were flushed, and I could see he was having one of the best times of his life.

The way it finally turned out, the three of us had a pretty nice afternoon, I must admit. First we walked up to the bus terminal at 42nd Street where we checked my suitcase in a luggage locker. Then we strolled over toward the Hudson River and got on this three-hour boatride all around Manhattan Island. It was a bright, sunny day with a breeze blowing, and somehow New York and its surroundings didn't look as polluted from down on the water as they had from Midge's window. We bought hot dogs for lunch on the boat, and Arthur kept counting the bridges we passed under. He insisted there had been twenty of them, even though Peter and I both thought he was exaggerating a little.

"Maybe we went under the same bridge twice," I suggested.

"No, *sir*," Arthur roared. "I counted 'em, Teen. And I say *twenty*!"

"What Tina means," Peter said very softly, "is that maybe we went under different loops of the same bridge, so technically you could both be right."

But Arthur wouldn't be budged. He said it was twenty *different* bridges, so we left him alone and once, when he wasn't looking, Peter winked at me.

After the boatride, Peter said he'd have to go shopping for the food he needed for dinner, so we got my suitcase from the terminal and rode uptown on a bus, and Peter dropped us at the Museum of Natural History because it was close enough to the apartment for Arthur and me to walk home.

Naturally, Arthur made a beeline for the top floor of the museum where the dinosaur skulls and other bones were kept. I knew he would, because we'd been there before some time ago with Midge, before she went to Mexico. The moment we got up to the fourth floor I was sorry we hadn't gone straight home or even food shopping with Peter.

"How much longer do you expect to go on looking at this thing?" I asked Arthur, after tagging along behind him while he spent nearly ten minutes just examining one side of a tremendous skeleton of a brontosaurus that was supposed to be about 193 million years old.

He half turned. "Well, give me a chance, can't you, Teen? I haven't seen it for a while. It's a vegetarian, you know."

"Oh, really," I remarked disinterestedly. "And has it grown any since your last visit?"

Arthur ignored that. "This old bronto," he said familiarly, "is about seventy feet long. And that other guy you see behind him" — he pointed to a much smaller dinosaur skeleton in back — "is chasing him because he wants to eat him up. He's called an allosaurus, and he's one of the first meat-eating dinosaurs there was."

I stepped between Arthur and the dinosaurs. "All right," I said. "I can see you're hooked and I wouldn't want to tear you away from your old buddies. So how about we make a deal?"

Arthur looked at me sharply. "What kind of deal?"

"Well, I'm bored with all these dry bones. I guess I just haven't got your vivid imagination. So suppose I go off to the South Pacific section or the Mexican Indians or some place like that, and then I come back and pick you up at exactly four-thirty. Would that be okay?"

"Sure," Arthur said quickly. "That'd be fine. Except, if I'm not in here — this place is called the Early Dinosaurs Hall — I'll be in the Late Dinosaurs." He pointed. "It's just through there. You can't miss it."

I hesitated. Naturally I felt responsible for Arthur, and besides he suddenly looked so small there among all those enormous skeletons with fierce saw-edge teeth and spiked tails. Some of them even had terrifying sharp claws and scales that looked like bats' wings.

Arthur smiled sweetly. "It's okay, Teen. Really, I don't mind a bit. I'll be fine here. You just go ahead and enjoy yourself."

I began to feel even more nervous about leaving him. I bent over him. "Now listen, Arthur," I said firmly but softly, "I'm probably going to sound like Nana Tess, but I want you to promise me you won't talk to any strangers while you're here alone. And if anyone does come and bother you . . . well, look over there in that corner where the guard is standing. Just march right over to him and tell him if anything's wrong. Do you promise me you'll do that?"

Arthur nodded solemnly.

"And I'll come back for you at four-thirty sharp." We looked at each other's watches to make sure they were both going and that we both had the same time. "And you be sure to be in the *Late* Dinosaurs Hall." I pointed in the direction Arthur had indicated. "You ought to be through with the early dinosaurs by then, and it's better to have a definite meeting place."

Arthur nodded again, and I left him.

Most of the time away from Arthur, I

spent down on the second floor, wandering among the stone statues and carved pillars and burial tombs of the Aztecs and Mayas who had once lived in Mexico and Central America. It was dark and a little scary among the long rows of glass cases that held the smaller pieces of pottery and the jewelry and tiny figurines. But it made me feel pretty far away from home, which was fine.

The only time I thought about the Saturday Sad Souls Club was when I came across a group of giggly girls, about my age, staring at the funny-shaped bodies of some of the miniature stone figures of ancient Indian men and women. And for a moment I caught myself thinking that it would have been nice to have Ina with me so that we could whisper to each other about the different things we were looking at. But of course that was out of the question now. And to think that our big bust-up fight had taken place only yesterday!

I was beginning to wonder why I'd been so dead set against going to stay with Mom and Peter. So far I'd been having a really pleasant time. And Peter couldn't have been nicer to me. There was just one thing that had made me a little uncomfortable. Actually, it made me feel sorry for Peter (in the same way I'd started feeling sorry for Mom that first day at the apartment when she was trying to get reacquainted with Arthur and me), and that was when I noticed Peter counting his money when he thought nobody was noticing. Twice I saw him take out his wallet and carefully finger each bill, once when we were on the boat trip, just before lunch, and again when we were on the bus riding uptown.

It suddenly came to me that all of this entertainment for Arthur and me was probably costing him and Mom plenty. And I was pretty sure Mom wasn't taking any money from Pop, even to help pay for our long visit. According to what I'd heard, she was pretty proud and had never taken any money from him at all since the time she'd left him.

I finally decided I'd had enough wandering around among the long-ago Indians, so even though it wasn't quite time to meet Arthur, I started for the top floor of the museum. I suppose I was feeling a little nervous about having left Arthur on his own, and I was hoping I wouldn't have any trouble finding him once I got to the dinosaurs. Sure enough, he was there all right, in the Late Dinosaurs Hall. The only strange thing was that he was standing in front of a large display case, waving his arms around, pointing, and talking out loud.

I was shocked to see Arthur talking to himself. Could he have actually gone a little crazy from having been exposed to too many dinosaurs?

But when I got a little closer I could see that there *was* somebody standing at Arthur's side, to whom he seemed to be talking. It was somebody much taller than Arthur because every now and then Arthur would stop and tilt his head upward, cocking it slightly to one side. A ripple of panic ran through me. For a fleeting second or two I thought the person beside him might be Peter. Suppose he'd come looking for us and found out I'd left Arthur alone. I felt guilty. But the next moment I realized that it wasn't Peter at all. It was a tall, fair-haired young man who looked to me to be about eighteen. Now I was *really* getting annoyed with Arthur. Hadn't I *told* him not to talk to any strangers?

I walked straight up to the display case, which seemed to have a heap of some kind of dried leather in it. Arthur wasn't startled. He glanced at me very casually and went on talking to the tall young man — some nonsense about the thing in the case being a "dinosaur mummy," from Wyoming of all places.

"Arthur!" I exclaimed, hoping the tone of my voice would remind him of my earlier warning. Arthur broke off his conversation just long enough to say, "Okay, Tina. I see you." He glanced at his watch. "But it's not time yet. You're early." Then he turned back to his new friend, who was now staring and smiling at both of us, but especially at me. I looked at Arthur's friend more closely. He had large, even features and a long chin. His eyes were brown and had a straining, nearsighted look, and there was something very stiff and unnatural about the way he stood. He reminded me of a well-dressed department-store dummy.

"Excuse me," Arthur's companion said, smiling and bowing slightly from the waist. "I am Johann." He pronounced it *Yo-honn*. Then he extended his right hand to me to shake hands.

I was very surprised, but what could I do?

"My name is Tina," I said. And we shook hands.

Arthur looked up at him. "I'm Arthur," he said. "I guess I didn't tell you that. Tina, here, is my sister." And then Arthur and Johann shook hands.

Nobody seemed to know what to say next, and there was an awkward silence. Finally, staring hard at Arthur, I said, "Well, and how long have you two been talking, Arthur?" I spoke each word very loudly and clearly, hoping Arthur would get my message this time, about his having promised not to talk to anyone while I was gone.

But Arthur carried on as usual. "Oh, a while," he said vaguely. "You see, Teen — um — Johann here is an expert on dinosaurs 'n' stuff. And this thing here in the case that we've been talking about is a dinosaur *mummy*. Now that's very unusual, isn't it — um — Johann?"

Johann nodded vigorously. "Yes, extremely so. As you can see, it is a trachodont, a two-legged duck-billed dinosaur of the late period, perhaps 136 million years old. Ordinarily, as you know, we have only bone matter from these great reptiles surviving through the ages, but in this case due to a peculiar combination of soil composition and dry weather conditions, this specimen was preserved almost intact, offering us a fine opportunity to examine the hide, which, you can observe, is of very tough material indeed."

Arthur kept on nodding all through Johann's lecture. The words sounded stilted, with a touch of some sort of foreign accent, but Johann was certainly able to speak fluently in English once he got started. In fact, he sounded exactly like a college professor or at least a high-school geology teacher. I was beginning to understand, and even forgive, Arthur's reason for talking to him.

"I guess you must . . . work here at the museum," I ventured hesitantly.

Johann's moist brown eyes opened wider and he answered me with a short but unexpectedly loud laugh. "What? Me? Oh, no. It's very kind of you to think so. But I am too young, only sixteen. And, anyhow, I don't even live here. In New York, I mean. I am only visiting here."

"Oh, I see," I said slowly, thinking that he was certainly quite grownup-looking for his age. At the same time I was getting angry at Arthur again for picking up strangers in the museum. "Where *do* you live then?"

"In the Netherlands," he answered. "Holland, you know? In The Hague. It's an important city. Like Philadelphia or Boston."

I turned to Arthur. "Did you know that, Arthur?" I asked pointedly.

"Of course, I knew it," Arthur answered defiantly. But I couldn't be sure what part of Johann's statement Arthur was so certain of knowing.

I looked at my watch. It was twenty minutes past four. "Well, Arthur," I said, "I think you'll have to say good-by to Johann now. It's time for us to be going."

Johann took a jolting half-step forward. "Oh really? Must you be going? It's such a pleasure to find somebody to chat with. I don't know anybody else in New York."

I was a little taken aback. He really did seem very lonely.

"None of us *could* stay much longer," I remarked, glancing at the time again. "The museum closes at a quarter to five."

"Ah, yes, that's true," Johann said with a sigh. "The time goes so quickly when one is enjoying oneself."

We all began to walk toward the exit stairs.

"Are you going back to Holland now?" Arthur wanted to know.

"No," Johann laughed softly. "Just back to the hotel. I must meet my father there for dinner at six P.M."

"You're living in a hotel?" Arthur breathed. "That must be keen. I never did. Right now we're staying at . . ."

"Never mind, Arthur," I said, as we started down the steps. "I'm sure Johann isn't interested."

"Oh, but I am," he said. "It's pretty dull at the hotel. My father has business to attend to all day. And people in New York seem to be hurrying about all the time. I'm here four days now and Arthur is the first stranger I've become at all acquainted with."

We had come to the landing between floors. Arthur paused, looking pleased with himself. "What's your father's business?"

"Oh," Johann waved an arm, as we began walking down the steps again, "he's an art dealer. He comes to New York each year to buy and sell paintings, sculpture, antiques. None of that interests me very much. However, he decided this time to give me a treat in the school holidays and so he's brought me along with him. Myself, I'm like Arthur. I'm more interested in old bones."

"Ugh," I gasped. "Not for me."

"Tina hates old bones," Arthur said. "She has no imagination."

"Really, Arthur," I scolded. "You don't have to repeat everything I say."

Pretty soon we were down on the main floor of the museum, heading toward the 77th Street exit. "There is so much more to see here," Johann clucked, looking around longingly. "I should like to come back tomorrow. What about you?"

Although Johann seemed to be looking at me, I figured he was talking to Arthur. I looked at Arthur who shrugged, looking back at me. "*I* sure wouldn't mind," Arthur said, after a moment, "but maybe Peter's got something else planned for us to do."

"I don't know," I said shaking my head and thinking again about Peter secretly counting his money. "You probably don't realize it, Arthur, but these boatrides and things cost a heap of money. Museums at least are free or pretty cheap anyway."

Johann squared his shoulders and his generous mouth widened into a broad smile. "Is it definite then? Will I see you here tomorrow? What time then? One o'clock?"

Arthur scratched his head. "Yeah, probably. I'll be up in the dinosaurs looking around. Just in case I get there before you."

Johann stepped forward, stretching out both hands to me. "You too, Tina. Of course."

I was a little shocked. Something in his

voice, something I hadn't noticed there before, made me feel strangely uncomfortable. My nose twitched, just slightly. I backed away.

"Arthur already told you," I said. "I have no imagination when it comes to old bones."

"Of course," Johann answered warmly, "but that doesn't matter a bit. We'll find something you can enjoy, too. It's a very large museum." He turned to Arthur. "We'll find something all three of us can enjoy. Why not?"

"Maybe," Arthur said grudgingly. "Yeah, I s'pose so."

We were out on the street now. Arthur and I turned to go west, toward the river. Johann had to go downtown, alongside the park. "Good-by for now," Johann called out happily. "See you tomorrow. Don't forget please, Tina. One o'clock."

But he never left the spot where we'd parted. He stood there waving all the while Arthur and I were walking down the long street toward the avenue. I knew, because every time I turned around to look I could see his arms wheeling faster and faster, like a windmill in a sharp, whipping breeze.

By the time Arthur and I did turn the

corner and finally lose sight of him, I realized Johann's behavior — and especially his last few words to me — had given me a sensational case of twitching nostrils.

8

The apartment looked and smelled like a Chinese restaurant! The living room, where the table was set for dinner, was hung with paper lanterns, and the table itself had bamboo place mats, chopsticks, lacquer bowls, and small dishes of hot-yellow mustard and dark-red duck sauce on it. Mom, who had been hanging a papier-mâché Chinese dragon from the ceiling, jumped down to welcome us, especially me. She didn't say much, but she hugged me tightly, while Peter came out of the kitchen with a long wooden cooking spoon in his hand and stood in the doorway and beamed.

"Chinese food!" Arthur exclaimed, and he followed Peter back into the kitchen, sniffing like a puppy dog, while Wart, the real dog, remained seated indifferently in the living room. A few seconds later Arthur came out of the kitchen yelling, "Hey, Tina, come and see. Peter's got a wok!"

I turned to Mom and made a face. "What's *that*?" We were in one of the small, narrow rooms off the hallway, where Peter had parked my suitcase. Mom was folding up the Indian printed-cotton divan-cover and explaining that this was going to be my bedroom during my visit.

While she stood and watched, I began unpacking my suitcase — the two special, natural-bristle brushes I used for my hair, the manicure kit in the pale-blue leather case that Nana Tess had given me on my last birthday, and some eye shadow and face-blusher that I'd bought for demonstrations at Sad Souls meetings. Unfortunately, I'd left the fruit-flavored lip glosses and the transparent liquid face-makeup behind at

Amy's house on Saturday when I'd raced out in such a rush to avoid Karla.

Mom picked up the eye-shadow kit. It looked like a small paintbox with its twelve little round pots of color ranging from "bone-China white" to "black denim."

"What's this?" Mom asked, mildly surprised. "I didn't know you used makeup, Tina. I didn't think kids were into that sort of thing anymore."

I took a pair of thin summer pajamas out of the suitcase and laid them on the bed. "Some are, some aren't," I said. "Not heavy makeup. It isn't supposed to be noticeable. It's . . . well, it's just supposed to be *there*."

Mom wrinkled her forehead. "Why wear it then? If it isn't supposed to be noticeable?"

I straightened up. "Because it *is* supposed to make you look better, to bring out your best points. Didn't you ever look through *Teen Charm* magazine? They tell you all about that stuff. Every month."

Mom gently dropped the eye-makeup kit on the small table that served as a sort of desk-dresser with a mirror over it. She leaned against the wall and crossed her arms nonchalantly. "But, Tina, you're not a teen. You're only twelve."

"Not really," I corrected. "I'm in my

thirteenth year, and I'm starting junior high school in September, remember. *Everyone* there is a 'teen,' even if they're only eleven. In which case, heaven help them."

Mom flipped the long pigtail braid of her hair out behind her. It was a habit she had whenever she was impatient or faintly annoyed. "I can see that the suburbs haven't changed," she said softly.

I lifted a pair of jeans and two tops out of the suitcase and hung them on the pegs of the old-fashioned wooden clothes tree in the corner, which took the place of a closet. "I guess I know what you mean," I said thoughtfully. "But it's just natural, in a place where everybody goes to the same school and we all know one another, for everyone to talk and act and dress pretty much the same. Except each person tries to be just a little better than the next. If they can."

After all, I thought, wasn't that why I'd organized the Saturday Sad Souls Club? So we could each help one another to be "better"? Until Karla came along, that is. She was just *too* much better.

Mom, still leaning against the wall, crossed one sneakered foot over the other. "It all sounds suffocating to me and awfully competitive. Like a Miss America contest that never ends."

I finished unpacking and plopped down on the bed. "I guess you really hated it," I said, not daring to look up at Mom, "living out there. I admit it isn't like living in New York City, or in . . . in some place like Mexico, where you can do whatever you want and nobody thinks it's peculiar. But — well, for me — I've always lived in the suburbs. And I just don't think I could ever get used to doing things your way. In fact, I think the way . . . the way you live, you and Peter, is really sort of . . . strange." I paused, looking down at the floor. "Sorry, but I just had to say it."

Mom hopped over to the bed and sat down beside me. She didn't put her arm around me or anything like that. But she rubbed her shoulder against mine a few times in a friendly, warm way. "That's all right, Tina. We don't have to be the same, you and me. I call it 'being free to be yourself.' Peter and I both call it that. That's why we're okay together."

I nodded wordlessly, and we both sat there quietly for a while. Everything suddenly seemed a lot better between us. Not perfect, but better.

"Tina!" Arthur fairly screeched from somewhere along the corridor. "Are you or aren't you coming to see Peter cooking in his wok? And anyhow everything's 'most ready to eat. Chinese food can't stand around or it gets limp and soggy. That's what Peter just told me."

Mom and I turned to look at each other and we both smiled. Of all things, I discovered that we both had wet eyes. No tears, but I could see Mom's and I could feel mine.

"We're coming!" we called back in a chorus of two.

Mom stood up and tucked her shirt more tightly into her jeans. I looked into the mirror and brushed my hair a few strokes. "What's Arthur so excited about anyway?" I asked Mom. "What's a wok?"

Mom rolled back the sleeves of her shirt one more turn. "It's a Chinese cooking pot," she replied. "Looks like a big sloping basin. Makes Chinese dishes that taste like and are the real thing. You'll see."

I put the brush down on the dresser. "Where'd Peter . . . where'd he learn all this stuff about cooking?"

"Mostly he taught himself how," Mom said, as we started down the long hallway toward the living room. "Peter grew up in the South. His mother died when he was very young, and after a while, he used to come home from school and do the cooking for his father and his older brother who worked. By now he's so good at it, he's going to start teaching at a cooking school in a couple of weeks. And one of these days, he's going to open a school of his own."

"Really?" I breathed.

"Really," Mom assured me. She turned and looked straight in my eyes. "I'll bet Peter's not having a job was one of the things that was bothering you," she said.

I didn't like to say anything so I just shrugged.

Mom laughed. "Of course, it was," she said. "It's okay. You don't have to be afraid to admit it!"

Arthur had nearly finished his heaping portions of almond chicken and beef with snow peas when he finally took the time to look up and admire the papier-mâché Chinese dragon that was hanging above the table. It turned out that Mom had made it down at the studio, and she was going to give it to us to take back to Nana Tess's if we wanted it.

I let my eyes slide past the fierce yellow

eyes and the giant nostrils, like two red fire-holes, and along the snaky body that was covered with bright green scales tipped with gold. "That dragon reminds me," I mused, "of one of Arthur's monsters over at the museum."

Arthur drew himself up and looked insulted. "One of *my* dinosaurs?"

"Yes. Well, not the way they look now, of course. Now they're just heaps of bones and a little dried skin." I was thinking of the dinosaur mummy from Wyoming. "But the way they might have looked when they were young and fresh and juicy."

Arthur banged the table in indignation. "Never!" he declared. "They didn't look anything like that. Those fellas were really *something*. They were something like *you* never saw."

"And neither did you," I reminded him.

"What Tina probably means," Peter offered, acting the peacemaker again, "is that dragons look a lot like giant lizards, which is what dinosaurs really were. So maybe, somehow, a description of them came down to early man and was passed on through drawings and legends."

Arthur helped himself to some more almond chicken, picking out, I noticed, as many almonds as he could along the way.

"I doubt that," he said. "Everybody knows the last dinosaurs died over forty million years before the first people — if you could call them that — came crawling around. But anyhow, just to show you I'm open-minded, I'll ask Johann about that tomorrow."

"Who is Johann?" Mom inquired, filling Peter's teacup and then her own with Chinese tea.

"He's this fellow I met at the museum today," Arthur replied, picking an almond out of the serving bowl and popping it into his mouth when he thought nobody was looking. "Well, actually Tina met him, too, but I'm the one who met him first."

"He's from Holland," I added. "Just visiting."

"And he likes Tina a lot," Arthur added. "I could tell."

I turned sharply to Arthur, my nose giving a single twitch. "Now why'd you say that?" I demanded.

Arthur shrugged. "He does. He kept begging you to show up at the museum tomorrow. He even said we'd go look at something else besides dinosaurs because you don't like them."

I turned back to the food on my plate. "Well, you don't have to worry about that," I said, hoping I sounded really aloof, "because I just might not join you."

Arthur looked up in shock. "Why not?"

"I just told you why. I don't want to spoil your fun. And besides, Johann . . . well, he makes me feel funny. Maybe we both ought to go to some other museum."

"We can't," Arthur said flatly. "We promised."

"How old is Johann?" Mom asked quietly.

"He's sixteen," I said. "But at first I thought he was about eighteen. It isn't his age, it's his looks. I mean . . . he *looks* all right. He's tall and his face is okay, but he's so . . . stiff and awkward. Even his clothes. They're the right kind of clothes, and yet . . . they don't look right. Oh," I added impatiently, "I can't explain."

"His father's an art dealer. He buys and sells paintings 'n' stuff," Arthur cut in, and he told Mom and Peter all about how Johann had happened to come to New York and how he was staying at a hotel. "He's really an okay guy," Arthur went on. "And he's sort of handsome, too. I don't know why Tina doesn't like him. I even thought she did."

"Well, sorry to have to correct you. But I do not."

Mom looked from Arthur to me. "I'm confused, too. Johann sounds lonely and he probably just wants to be with some people fairly close to his own age. Would it be so awful to spend a few hours with him in the museum?"

"I suppose not," I said, feeling my cheeks flush and my nostrils getting dryer.

"Well, then, why not meet him tomorrow? I thought the reason teen-age girls tried to make themselves attractive was to attract teen-age boys. Now you've attracted one and you don't seem to be interested. How come?"

I leaned my elbow on the table and rested my chin on my hand. I was still trying to sort out my confused feelings. "It's because he's sort of . . . well, creepy . . . and now I feel that way, too. I mean, about seeing him again. I just wouldn't know how to act with him."

"You acted fine with him today," Arthur piped up. "You were just yourself, and that's when he started to like you."

"That's the whole trouble," I said quickly, putting my hand back down in my lap. "He changed it all when he started to like me. Now . . . well, now I'd feel so self-conscious

I wouldn't know what to say to him. I couldn't. Anyhow, I look terrible and I didn't bring any nice clothes."

"Looks, looks, looks," Arthur said disgustedly. He turned to Mom and Peter. "Did you know Tina takes her glasses off when Nana Tess isn't around? She did it on the train the last time we came here."

"Oh, be still, Arthur," I said irritably. "Why must you always tell tales?"

"But I'm trying to *tell* you," Arthur persisted, turning back to me, "that you were wearing your glasses this afternoon. And your old clothes. And you looked just the same as you do now. And Johann liked you."

"The reason he 'liked' me," I started to explain to Arthur, as patiently as I could, "is because . . . because Johann would have a lot of trouble getting a . . . well, a really great-looking, attractive girl to go out with him. Because he is, after all, a little . . . strange-looking and strange-acting.

I suppose I was thinking of someone like Karla when I said that. Would *she* have gone out with Johann? No, Tiger Rawson was more her type. And certainly, as to appearances, I couldn't think of two more perfect-looking people. It was the way Cokie Adams had said it was, in her last letter from camp

—all the cute-looking boys were "taken" by the popular girls. All the other girls were leftovers and had to make do with whatever boys were left over. And I hated the idea of being a leftover. I was still hoping I wouldn't be. And yet . . . I was, I was. What else was I? Didn't Johann's liking me *prove* that I was?

Peter, with that uncanny way he seemed to have of reading my mind, leaned across the table. His bland, pale face was still shining with sweat from cooking in the hot apartment kitchen. "Tina, even if there were something wrong with your looks — which there isn't — you don't really believe that looks are all that important, do you?"

That was a ticklish question. I glanced at Mom. Was Peter trying to tell me that Mom looked fine in her wire-rim glasses, her hair pulled back tight, not the tiniest bit of make-up, and that he liked her that way? Well, maybe he did but I *still* knew she could look better — much, much better.

"I do think looks are important," I said, breathing a little harder. "A lot of people could look much more attractive than they do. After all, it's the first thing you see when you meet a person, isn't it? How would you ever find out if somebody had a lovely personality or a beautiful soul, or whatever, if they were so ugly looking that you passed them right by and never got to know them?"

"Aha!" Peter said, smiling but pointing a pudgy finger directly at me. "Now you've said it. So why don't you give Johann a chance? He wants to give you one. Not that I'm saying that either of you is the least *bit* ugly looking. But then you're not a pair of glamorous movie stars either. Right?"

I sighed, half agreeing.

"And I'll tell you one thing more," Peter said, "because I'm very Chinese and therefore very wise tonight. Keep your glasses on, Tina, when you meet Johann. Because the important thing is to see *him*. If you concentrate on the other person, you'll forget about yourself and you won't be nearly so self-conscious. He'll like it better, too. I guarantee it." Peter turned to Mom. "Right?"

Mom looked back at him. "Right!" she said, playfully pounding the edge of the table with her fist. And then they both winked at each other through their glinting, metal-framed eyeglasses.

Just as we were finishing dessert (kumquat ice cream, which Peter said he made himself by mixing chopped preserved kumquats into vanilla ice cream), I got two phone calls. One was from Pop, who also talked to Arthur for a while. The other one was from, of all people, Amy.

Everything she said sounded like it ended in a question mark. I guess she was worried I wouldn't want to talk to her because of my fight with Ina.

"Tina? It's Amy?"

"Oh, hi." I was surprised but wary. "How'd you know I was here? How'd you get this number?"

"From your father?"

"My father? That's funny. I just talked to my father and he didn't say you phoned."

"Well, I didn't actually. I think it was Mrs. Philips who phoned him?"

"Oh?"

"Well, she was worried about you, Tina. I guess Ina told her you and she had some kind of a ... ?"

"Fight," I said emphatically.

"Yes ... fight," Amy repeated, "and she — Mrs. Philips — didn't know if there was anybody to take care of you?"

"There are plenty of people to take care of me," I retorted, "including myself, of course."

"Of course," Amy agreed meekly.

There was a pause.

"You're not angry at *me*, are you, Tina? Because it wasn't us who had the fight."

I didn't answer that directly. "I can tell that Ina was the one who gave you this telephone number. And did she also tell you what we argued about?"

"Well, sort of. But Tina, I had nothing to do with it. And I had nothing to do with Tiger calling you that . . . name on Saturday."

"Nothing? Well, maybe not. But you were the one who brought Karla into the SSSC, and that's what started all the trouble. Just remember that."

"Oh, that reminds me, Tina. About Karla."

"What about Karla?"

"Well, I wasn't going to tell you this, but maybe I should. I found out something. Even Ina doesn't know it yet. It's about Karla."

"You already said that. What about Karla?"

"Well, like I said, I only just found out about it this afternoon when I was over at Karla's house. And, I honestly do think maybe, as president of the club, you should know it."

"Well, *tell* me already."

"Okay, I'm telling. See, we were in Karla's

room, just she and I, playing some records of her brother's. And she happened to open this drawer in her dresser, and I looked in and it had all these hundreds of pencils and erasers and ball points and rolls of Scotch tape and so forth in it."

"Stuff she shoplifted."

"Right. Only the trouble is — well, I don't know how to tell you this, Tina, but — she didn't!"

"What do you mean 'she didn't'?"

"She didn't shoplift that stuff."

"How do you know?"

"Because when I saw all those things sitting there in her drawer, I said, 'Karla, I thought you kept that stuff hidden away. What if your mother came in to clean or look for something and she opened that drawer and saw all that? Wouldn't she be suspicious or anything?' And Karla just looked at me and she laughed."

"She laughed?"

"Right. She just laughed. And then she said she wasn't the least bit worried because she'd never stolen it in the first place."

"Do you mean to tell me that she actually *lied* to us about being a kleptomaniac? She's not a kleptomaniac at all?"

"That's right, Tina. Isn't it awful?"

"Where'd she say she got all those things then? How could you be sure she wasn't lying about that?"

"Because the answer is simple, Tina. Her father brings it home. He's an office manager for some big company, and they buy stationery and office supplies by the carload. She admitted that she only told me she stole it because she needed to have some kind of a problem to get into the SSSC, and there wasn't anything wrong with her looks except her freckles. And there wasn't even anything wrong with them."

"Oh, really, Amy," I groaned. "That is *too* much. You honestly mean to tell me that she never, never stole anything. Not even when she was going with that crowd in New York that used to shoplift for kicks?"

"I asked her that, too."

"And what did she say?"

"She said she once took a tiny bottle of Sparkling Grape nail polish and a package of emery boards off the counter. But she only walked around the store with them and put them back before she left."

"What a terrible liar, trying to get into the club under false pretenses." I was getting more and more outraged at Karla. "Weren't you furious with her?"

"I . . . I didn't have a chance. She kept giggling and she said it was only a white lie because she was new in the neighborhood and wanted to make friends quickly and that seemed the only way. She said she thought that deep down we all understood it was a joke about her kleptomania."

"Some joke. The joke was on us. It shows the kind of person Karla really is. You aren't still going to her party, are you, Amy?"

There was complete silence at the other end.

"Amy?"

"Yes, did you say something, Tina?"

"I *said*, now that you found out what a liar Karla is, are you still going to her party Friday night?"

"Well, actually . . . oh, I don't know, Tina. It sounds like a really fun party. Ina's going. I live right next door to Karla. How could I not go?"

"You're going then."

"Well, I guess."

"Amy, you have no spine."

"I wish you'd come too, Tina. Karla mentioned you again this afternoon. She says you're still invited. You'd get to meet some boys, Tina. And Karla's brother is going to be there. . . ."

"Thank you, Amy," I said hotly, surprising even myself, "but I've already met a boy right here in the city."

"You have?" Amy gasped. "So soon? You've only been there one day."

"I know," I said smugly. "Sometimes it doesn't take long at all. In fact, I have a date with him tomorrow afternoon at one o'clock, and actually I have to get off the phone now because I have to wash my hair. The air here in the city is just filthy. Well, of course, you could ask Karla about that. She lived in the city so she would know."

"Yes." Amy cleared her throat. "What's he like, Tina, this boy you have the date with?"

"*Very* cute," I said. "Tall, good looking, brown eyes and light-brown hair. He's sixteen, but he looks even older. When I first met him I actually thought he was eighteen."

"Oh, Tina." Amy breathed. "I don't know anybody sixteen. What's his name?"

"His name?"

"Yes, his name, Tina. What's his name? You know his name, don't you?"

"Well, of course I know his name. I was just thinking of something else for a moment. It's . . . Joe. Joe, that's short for . . . Joseph."

"Yes, I know it is," Amy said. "Listen,

maybe I can phone you tomorrow after your date and we can talk some more? I'm so excited about your boyfriend. It's just fantastic, Tina. I think you're the first one of us to have a boyfriend. Except for Karla, of course. I think she's had a few. Is it okay if I mention it around? Would you mind?"

"Oh, no," I said, choking suddenly on a bit of chewed almond that must have dropped out of my teeth and fallen into my throat. "I don't mind at all."

I hung up the phone and went to my room to get ready to wash my hair. But when I got there, I suddenly felt a little sick to my stomach. I sat down on the sagging divan in the dark for a few minutes, wondering what could be wrong with me.

My conversation with Amy had been a real triumph and a satisfaction, so it couldn't be that. I finally decided it had to be Peter's cooking. Kumquat ice cream. Really!

9

"Tina, are you coming *ever?* It's a quarter to one already."

Arthur was standing in the doorway of my room at Mom and Peter's. Mom was at work and Peter, who was on his way to school, was going to go down in the elevator with us. Peter was actually taking a course in butchering and meat-cutting, as training for his teaching job at the cooking school, and it met every Tuesday afternoon.

My hair was a mess. It was too fluffy and full of both corkscrew snarls and long tangles. It must have been the shampoo Mom had lent me, which made it too dry or something. Or maybe it was the water. I hadn't brought along my own shampoo because there was only a little bit left in the big bottle at home, and I'd figured I'd buy a fresh one in New York City when I needed it.

"Arthur, be reasonable. I can't leave this room with two combs and a brush caught in my hair. So you'll just have to be patient a few more minutes."

"I don't see why you had to wash it anyway. It looked fine yesterday. Would you like me to get you a scissors? You could cut out the snarls where the combs are caught. There's so much of it, nobody would ever know."

I gave a short, tight screech at the very thought. "No, and don't you ever mention that word to me again."

"You mean scissors?"

"Ar-*thur*, I'm warning you . . ." My screech had brought both Peter and Wart to the door of my room. Peter had just brought the dog back from his walk and now he had his notebook under his arm, ready to leave for class.

It was hopeless, I knew, to keep at my hair. After pulling out the combs and the brush, there were three big extra-frizzy puffs that I had to pat back in place with my hands as best I could.

On the way down in the elevator, Peter handed me a set of keys to the apartment. "You can be in charge of these, Tina, just in case I'm delayed for any reason and you two should get back from the museum before me. But I honestly prefer you don't use the elevator alone or let yourselves into the apartment when no one's there, even though Wart will set up a howl. I should be back by four-thirty for sure."

I took the keys from Peter, and we all went out into the street and walked to the corner where Peter reminded me, with a wink, to keep my glasses on and have fun. Then he caught his bus for downtown, and Arthur and I headed for the museum on foot.

It was one of those hot, sticky days with a veiled sun and mean little blasts of warm air swirling piles of dust and wastepaper around in whirlpools in the street. The humidity must have been close to one hundred per cent. We had crossed a couple of avenues when Arthur and I passed a drugstore that had a display of hand mirrors in the window, and I slowed down to catch my reflection in one of them. The sight was so horrifying that I stopped altogether.

"Arthur, just *look* at me!"

Arthur looked. "What's wrong? You look okay. Come on, it's after one. We're late."

"No, just look at me in the mirror."

"I don't get it. You look the same in the mirror as you do standing here in the street."

"I do? That's awful."

"Well, of course you do. What's wrong with you, Teen? Come on, let's go."

We started walking again, Arthur marching ahead and me lagging slightly behind now. "Arthur," I panted. "I can't."

He half turned. "Can't what? Come on, Teen. It's only a little further. See, there's the back of it now. That part's the Planetarium. I want to go there, too, one of these days. There's an entrance into the museum right near the Planetarium, so let's go that way. It'll be shorter. Boy, Johann must be wondering what happend to us."

He was even farther ahead of me now. "Arthur," I said suddenly, "I'm not going with you."

He stopped and whirled around in surprise. "What? What's wrong? You sick or something, Teen?"

"Well, in a way." I put my hands to my head. "Look at this hair. It's even worse now than when we left the apartment. It's this damp, hot wind. Well, I mean, it's . . . impossible. I can't face . . . anybody this way." I was feeling close to tears. "And I only wanted to look a little . . . better."

Arthur shifted from one leg to the other. I could see he was very uncomfortable. "Oh, for crying out loud, Teen. Maybe you should cut it all off."

I stamped my foot and shrilled at him. "Don't you *dare* say that to me. Don't you dare!"

We stood glaring at one another. Finally, I calmed down a little and started to think. "Look, Arthur, I'll walk you to the entrance just to make sure you get into the building all right. Then you go upstairs and meet — meet Johann. And be sure not to leave the museum building no matter what. Go look at anything you like inside, and I'll come back and pick you up at exactly four-thirty, just like yesterday. And in the exact same place. In the Late Dinosaurs, in front of the case with the mummy in it. Okay?"

Arthur scratched his head. "Well, okay. But what are *you* gonna do?"

"Don't worry about me. I'm going to walk

back to the apartment and stop at that drugstore on the way and buy a bottle of my regular shampoo, the kind I always use. Then I'm going upstairs to wash my hair and let it dry, and then I'll come back here and pick you up like I said. Is that clear?"

We were walking toward the museum entrance now, faster and faster. At the doorway Arthur said, "But you'll be alone in the elevator. Twice. Going up and going down. And Peter said we shouldn't."

"I told you, don't worry." I was breathless from the heat and the fast walking. "I'll be careful. I'll look for someone we know, and I'll get in the elevator when they do."

"But we don't know anybody," Arthur said with a helpless air.

I put my hands on his shoulders. "It's all right, Arthur. Now trust me."

"And what should I tell Johann," he asked, "about why you didn't show up?"

I dropped my hands. "Just tell him . . . tell him . . . Oh, tell him something came up and I couldn't make it."

Arthur raised his eyes to the frizzled-out halo of my hair and grinned. "Yeah, something came up, all right. Your hair. It's really headed for outer space, isn't it?"

"Arthur," I hissed, "don't you dare to tell him the truth. Do you understand me?"

His expression grew sober again and he nodded.

"And I'll meet you at four-thirty. Wait there for me, no matter what."

Arthur looked at his watch. "Hey, it's nearly one-thirty now! Am I ever late." And he flashed an arm at me and disappeared inside the museum.

The man in the drugstore didn't have the brand of shampoo I wanted and he tried to sell me another kind. I always felt shy with storekeepers and clerks, so it took me a little while to wriggle my way out of there and stop in another store where I finally got it.

By the time I reached the apartment building, I was really hot and tired, and it was getting late. I was in too much of a hurry to stand around waiting for some nice older lady to come along and get in the elevator with me. So, I just peeked into all four corners of the car before I got in, to make sure it was empty, and then stood in the middle clutching my package and praying no one would get on until I got to our floor. It was nice of Arthur to be so genuinely worried about me. I knew he was thinking of all those stories we'd heard about people being robbed and beaten up in self-service elevators in New York City. But I'd been feeling so desperate I hadn't been letting myself think about it much. Until this minute, anyway.

What a mess I'd gotten myself into, building up Johann to Amy, telling her I had a "date" with him, letting her call him my "boyfriend." He was nothing of the kind. He was just a lonely person trying to pass the time in a strange place where he didn't know anybody much. In fact, if you changed the "he" to a "she" that was almost an exact description of me!

As I stepped out of the elevator and the door clanged shut behind me, I could hear Wart setting up a growling and barking campaign inside the apartment, just as Peter had predicted he would. I had to keep talking to him through the slit in the doorway while I was getting the inside chain unlocked, hoping he wouldn't jump me when I finally got inside. Actually, he didn't stop barking until I'd closed the door behind me *and* put the chain back across the door. He was a pretty smart dog. After that, he just went back to his favorite place on the living room floor and ignored me.

After I finished washing my hair with the

new shampoo, there was nothing to do but watch television, combing my hair all the while it was drying so it wouldn't have a single chance to knot up. The television show was an old movie about a mining engineer and an archaeologist in the green jungles of South America. The archaeologist was a beautiful woman with buttery-smooth, pale-blonde hair that was never the least bit mussed up or frizzy, which was of course ridiculous because you can imagine how hot and humid it must be in a place like that.

Most of the time, though, I guess I wasn't paying much attention to the picture. I kept thinking about Arthur, hoping he was all right, wondering if it really was okay for him to meet Johann all by himself this afternoon. After all, what did we really know about Johann? He seemed nice enough, simple and honest. But there *were* people who looked so meek and kind, they wouldn't hurt a fly and who turned out to be child murderers! Maybe Mom and Peter were too easygoing. I had the feeling Nana Tess would never have let Arthur and me go to the museum alone to meet Johann. And that was the worst part of it. I hadn't even gone along with Arthur. I'd let him go alone.

My hair was taking forever to dry and I

didn't dare use Mom's blow-dryer on it for fear the corkscrews would come back. So, at four o'clock, I put a scarf on my head, tied it tightly under my chin, and started for the museum. This time there were two little old ladies going down in the elevator, and I got in with them. But we kept looking at each other suspiciously all the way down.

I'd suddenly remembered, after the elevator door had closed, about a murder story I'd heard of in which two sweet, elderly sisters had poisoned a whole bunch of old men and buried their bodies in the cellar. And, who knows, maybe *they* were thinking of some story they'd heard in which a tall, skinny, nearly teen-age girl, disguised in eyeglasses and a dark brown headscarf, had done away with two little old ladies by putting a spell on them and then stuffing their bodies into an elevator shaft. You couldn't trust anybody these days.

I forgot to use Arthur's "short cut" to get to the museum because I hadn't been paying much attention to anything but my hair on the way over. Instead, I found myself walking the same way Arthur and I had walked yesterday afternoon after leaving Johann, so I began speeding up as I approached the entrance because I was getting more and more anxious to make sure Arthur was okay. Even the fact that I was probably going to have to face Johann once I got there didn't seem to bother me as much now. Of course, there was also the chance that Johann had never shown up at all, in which case Arthur would have been alone in the museum all afternoon. Somehow that possibility bothered me even more.

By the time I'd climbed up the three long flights of stairs to the Late Dinosaurs Hall, I was really winded. But the elevators took forever to come, and when they did, they were always crowded. Except for a cluster of people around the huge tyrannosaurus skeleton in the middle of the room, the place was nearly deserted. A guard was standing over in the corner, his arms folded and his chin resting on his chest. He looked as though he'd fallen asleep standing up. There was no one at all over near the dinosaur-mummy case. But I went and stood there anyway. Of course, I was early. It was exactly a quarter past four.

I took off my scarf because my head felt so hot. My hair seemed to be wetter than before and plastered to my head. I suppose it looked as unbecoming as the wild frizz I'd had earlier that day, but there wasn't a single thing I could do about it. Besides, my mind was mostly on Arthur now. I still had fifteen minutes to wait, and I hoped he wouldn't be late.

I couldn't have been standing beside the dinosaur-mummy case for more than two or three minutes when Johann suddenly appeared, walking quickly toward me in long, hard strides. The moment I spotted him, all my nervousness about seeing him returned. One hand flew to the flat, wet hair at the side of my head and my nose began to twitch. My cheeks grew fiery as I thought of my ridiculous conversation with Amy last night. Boyfriend! Date! Really.

Johann came up to me with an eager expression on his face, reached out both hands and grasped my arms just above the elbows. "Tina, I'm so glad to find you here. Have you been waiting long?"

"N – no," I stammered. "I j – just got here a few minutes ago. I suppose I'm early. Arthur was supposed to meet me here at four-thirty."

"Yes," Johann said, looking, I thought, a little uncomfortable. "I know. He told me."

"I . . . I'm sorry I couldn't spend the afternoon with . . . with both of you," I said apologetically. At the same time I was wondering

why Johann kept looking around the room
and why Arthur wasn't with him. "Where's
Arthur?" I asked. "Didn't you and he stay
together this afternoon?"

Johann turned to me. His brown eyes
looked very bright and anxious. "We did.
Yes, yes, in fact, we did. We were together
for some time."

"Oh," I said, slightly puzzled, "and then I
guess you decided to go look at different
things." I glanced at my watch. "Well, he
still has about ten minutes to go, so I suppose he's taking his time."

Johann consulted his own watch. "Yes,
yes. I suppose he is. That must be it. He
knows he still has some time. But still, I
wonder, where can he be?"

I looked directly into Johann's eyes, which
were blinking rapidly now. "What do you
mean 'where can he be'? Don't you know
where he went?"

Johann looked solemn and pulled at the tip
of his ear. "To tell you the truth, Tina, I
thought he went here."

"What do you mean 'thought'?" I asked
uneasily. "When you two separated, didn't he
give you any idea of where he was going?"

Johann wheeled around on his heels, surveying the room and peering anxiously toward all the entrances.

"Johann," I said, using his name for the very first time and remembering, with so much embarrassment that my nostrils twitched frantically, how I'd lied and told Amy his name was Joe, "please tell me what this is all about. I think you're pretty worried about Arthur and I don't understand why exactly. Because he still does have a little time left and I know how Arthur is. He's very curious and he might have stopped to look at something that interested him on the way. He might even be over in the Early Dinosaurs, except I think it's better to stay and wait for him here because otherwise we might miss him and it would all turn into a mess."

Johann's face relaxed slightly. "Yes, of course, Tina. You are right. He is your brother and you know his ways. That is exactly what must have happened after he left me at the Planetarium."

"The Planetarium?" I said, surprised.

"Yes." Johann rubbed his hands. "That is where we went. After meeting and looking at some of the exhibits on the other floors for a while, Arthur mentioned that he had never been to the Planetarium. I had not been

155

either, and since it is really a part of the museum and actually connected to it, I said, 'Why not? Let's go.' I had enough money to pay for both of us."

"And then what?" I asked.

"Well, then we simply went. It was too early for the next performance of the sky show, which was to start at three-thirty, so we looked around at some of the Planetarium exhibits and they were very interesting — "

"Go on, go on," I broke in, hoping Johann wouldn't get side-tracked onto some astronomical subject and go into a long-winded explanation of the stars, as he had about the dinosaurs yesterday.

"Yes, of course. Well, then when it was nearly time, we went into the theater for the sky show. We took our seats and then the lights went out and it became completely dark, and they flashed the scene of the heavens on the domed ceiling showing over eight thousand stars plus the sun and the moon and the planets. . . ."

"Yes, Johann, I know," I said urgently. "I've been to the Planetarium."

Johann looked at me. "Oh, sorry," he said. Then he added almost dreamily, "Still, I do wish you could have been with us, Tina."

"Johann," I begged, "please stick to the

subject. What happened after the show started?"

"Well, it was most interesting and we were both watching the skies and listening very carefully. Arthur was sitting in the aisle seat and I was sitting right next to him. I must admit I found it very entrancing. I had no idea how much time passed, although I had heard someone say that the entire show would last about forty-five minutes. Perhaps Arthur grew restless. I do not know. Anyway, he very suddenly whispered to me that he was going to leave. I asked him why, and he said, 'Because I have to meet Tina.' And the very next moment he was gone."

Johann paused, and this time we both craned our necks looking around the room for Arthur. It was easily half-past four now, but there was still no sign of him.

I was confused. "What time was that? When he left you at the Planetarium, I mean?"

Johann screwed up his eyes. "I can't say exactly. You see, it was so dark in there. I tried to see my watch, but I couldn't. Perhaps it was about four o'clock. I began to think it was strange he should leave so soon because he had told me, when we met, that he had to meet you at four-thirty. And, as the show hadn't ended, I knew it couldn't be even four-fifteen yet."

"Maybe he had to go to the bathroom," I suggested. "Arthur eats like a pig sometimes. I mean, he just plain overeats." I was thinking of all of Peter's home-cooked Chinese food that Arthur had shoveled in the night before. And I remembered how even I had felt a little sick there for a while after talking to Amy. And I hadn't eaten half as much as Arthur.

"Yes," Johann said. "That thought came to me, too. So after a few more minutes, I got up and left too. The show had still not ended. I looked around carefully for him, in the bathroom and then in the exhibit halls just outside the auditorium, thinking he might have discovered he still had some time and stopped to look around a bit more. But there was no sign of him so I decided to come over here. Because he did say he was going 'to meet Tina.' " Johann looked around carefully once again. "But where is he? It is now" — he bent his head intently over his wristwatch — "exactly four . . . thirty-four . . . and three-quarters."

Johann seemed to be worrying enough for both of us. I almost felt like reaching out to pat his arm. "Let's not give up," I said, trying to sound hopeful for Johann's sake. "He'll probably turn up any minute now."

"I hope so," Johann replied with a heavy sigh. "You see, Tina, I do feel . . . well, responsible. He is, after all, a small boy. And I feel he was in my trust."

"Not really," I corrected him. "Actually, Arthur was in *my* trust, so I'm the one who's responsible. And honestly, Johann," I added, still trying to sound confident, "I'm not really worried. Yet."

But deep inside me, at the very pit of my stomach, there was a tiny worm of growing uneasiness that was beginning to squirm around more and more restlessly. Where *had* Arthur been for the past thirty-five or forty minutes? And where was he now?

10

"Sorry, Sis. Museum's closing now. Gonna have to ask you to leave."

It was the gray-uniformed guard from the corner of the Late Dinosaurs Hall. He had awakened from his stand-up sleep.

The last few stragglers were just disappearing out the exit, but I was still at my post, waiting now for both Johann *and* Arthur. Johann had gone to look for Arthur in the Early Dinosaurs Hall, just in case he was loitering in there for some reason. Arthur still hadn't shown up and it was now a quarter to five.

"But I can't leave here," I told the guard, beginning to have visions of chaining myself to the display case, "because I'm waiting for my brother. I'm beginning to think . . . I'm beginning to think he's lost."

The guard shook his head with a faint air of exasperation. "Now why didn't you watch over him? Where's he supposed to be, young lady?"

I began to feel awful. The guard's words weren't unkind, but his voice had a gruff quality and there was a sour twang to it. My nose twitched and a lump rose in my throat.

"Here," I said painfully. "He was supposed to meet me right here at four-thirty."

There was a sound of footsteps and the guard turned. "Well, here he comes now," he said, "so that settles that. I said we were closing and we are."

But, of course, it wasn't Arthur who was just coming into the room. It was Johann. He look distressed. "He's not in the Early Dinosaurs either, Tina. I looked. Everyone seems to be gone."

The guard, who had walked a few paces away, turned around.

"You two are gonna both have to leave. Right now."

"But this isn't my brother," I implored. "It's my . . . my brother's friend. We're waiting for my brother. He's only nine. And small. Well, short, anyway."

The guard spread both hands in front of him, palms up, and addressed his remarks to Johann. "Look, I can't help you, fella. The place is clearing out, so the kid couldn't get in here now anyway. Where was he when you last saw him?"

Johann was nervously clicking his thumbnail against the nail of his fourth finger, making a sharp, snapping sound. "The last time I saw him," he said, "was in the Planetarium."

"The Planetarium!" The guard threw up his hands. "Well, why don't you go and look for him down there? These little kids get excited about the different exhibits they've got — rockets, space capsules — hang around there for hours. And then they've got what they call that 'black light' gallery, showing the moon's surface and such. Real dark and scary. He's probably hiding out there for a laugh. Plenty of kids do. Oh, boy, do they give us a headache."

I glanced doubtfully at Johann. "That doesn't sound a bit like Arthur."

"But we could try there, Tina." His voice had a note of very faint hope. He turned to the guard. "And if he does come here, please tell him we've gone to meet him there, will you?"

The guard started walking us toward the exit, both hands lowered now, palms outward and moving up and back as if in a gentle shoving motion. "Sure, sure. I'll tell him."

"His name's Arthur," I said, stopping and taking one last look around. "Arthur Carstairs. And he's nine."

"Don't worry, Sis. I'll send him down to the Planetarium the minute I see him."

But I didn't feel very confident, and as Johann and I started glumly toward the staircase, we heard the guard call out to someone in a brisk voice, "Hey, Harry! All clear in here. I'm going off the floor."

A voice like a faint echo called back, "Gotcha, Fred."

And Fred, who'd promised us to keep watch for Arthur, called back even more faintly, "G'night, Harry." Then there was silence.

I turned mournfully to Johann. "Don't

worry, Tina," he said softly. "We'll find him. I'm sure of it. And I'll stay by your side until we do."

Down on the main floor of the museum, we headed straight for the entrance to the Planetarium. But of course the moment we got there, we were stopped by a guard. This one was tall and young, with long black hair sticking out from under his cap and a jutting lower jaw. "Planetarium's closed," he snapped. "Out that way." And he pointed toward the exit to the street.

"But we think my brother's in there," I protested in a tight voice. "Couldn't we just go in there and look?"

The guard folded his arms and grinned. He looked from Johann to me and then back at Johann again. "Oh, yeah?"

Johann stepped forward. "It's not something meant to be funny," he said with a tense air. "It isn't that we're trying to get in free or something like that. I was in there with this boy during the three-thirty sky show and he vanished from the theater at about four o'clock. Got up from his seat and he hasn't been seen since."

The guard rocked forward on the balls of his feet. "Look, I guarantee ya, the auditorium was cleared over half an hour ago. There's no one in there."

Johann and I both began to speak at once. "B...b...but..."

I let Johann take over. "But perhaps he is in the exhibit area. He could be" — Johann turned to me and gave me a meaningful look — "he could be hiding somewhere in the dark. These children do this sometimes, just to be mischievous. It's better to let us look, don't you think?"

The guard unfolded his arms and clapped his large hands to his thighs. "Nobody has to go in and look," he said. "We have a special system for that. You two stay right where you are, and I'll request a special-search-and-report. How old's this kid and what's his name?"

We told him and he went over to a recess in the wall near his post, reached in, and spoke into a small telephone. Johann and I waited nervously, not daring to look at each other. About two minutes later, the guard was back. "Planetarium's all clear, everybody's out, and it's locked up for the night. Museum's closed, too. Out the main entrance. Straight ahead and to your left." And he pointed the way with one of his long, swinging arms. Helplessly, we obeyed.

A few moments later we were out in the street, standing in front of the museum on Central Park West, in the warm, soupy New York City air. I bit hard at my lower lip and looked at Johann. "Suppose," I said, with the faintest stirring of hope, "suppose Arthur did hang around the Planetarium for a while after he left the sky show and then tried to get upstairs to meet me but couldn't because it was already too near closing time. And the guard just pointed him toward the exit the way he did us."

Johann leaned forward. "Yes?"

"Well, maybe he came out here onto the street like us, but then he figured *we* would be coming out one of the other exits, like yesterday when we all left by the side entrance at 77th Street. So he went around that way to look for us."

Johann's face lit up. "Yes, of course. That's a good possibility. Tina, why don't you stay here in case he still turns up at this entrance, and I will go around to that side and see if he's there. Then we will meet again right here."

I almost hated to see Johann walk away, even though I knew he would be coming back. Suppose he came back without Arthur? Then what? I went and sat down on one of the stone steps of the museum, my chin resting in my hands, to wait. The street below me was full of auto traffic, of people getting on and off buses and pouring in and out of the subway entrances. Arthur was a small, insignificant dot among these masses of people. He could have been caught up and whirled away like a speck of dust in the wind. And across the street from the museum was Central Park. It looked innocent enough from here, benches strung out facing the street against a background of dry, dusty shrubbery. But behind that shrubbery, in the depths of the park, terrible things were reported to be happening every day. I couldn't bear thinking about them. Suddenly, I longed for us both to be home, safe and sound, at Nana Tess's.

Even, I thought to myself, even if Tiger Rawson walked up to me the second I arrived and called me Tina the Teen-Age Twitch in front of a hundred junior high school kids, and Karla laughed in my face and looked up at Tiger, giggling and making eyes at how clever he was; even if Ina and I never spoke to each other again, and Amy found out the truth about Johann; even then I'd be happy and grateful to put up with it all, just knowing that Arthur was safe.

After about ten minutes, Johann returned. He was walking alone, quickly, and with his head down. The instant I spotted him, tears began pounding like a powerful surf behind my eyes. By the time he reached me, salty rivers were running down my cheeks and enormous drops were plopping onto the backs of my hands, which lay limply on my knees.

"Tina, Tina . . ." Johann bent over me gently. "Come on, let me take you home. The museum entrances are all shut tightly now. It's well past five o'clock."

I shook my head stubbornly back and forth, between deep, choking sobs. Johann placed a large, white handkerchief in my lap. It touched my hand and it felt soft and fine like the one Pop had pushed across the table to me at the Flying Dolphin. What a lot of crying I was doing these days! If this was what being a teen-ager was going to be like, it was going to be awful.

"I c . . . can't go home. What would I say to m . . . m . . . my parents? How could I tell them that I . . . I lost Arthur?" I looked up at Johann, blotting my eyes shakily with the handkerchief he'd given me. "D . . . don't you see that it's all my fault? I was never supposed to have left him by himself at the museum in the first place. Not even yester-day, when I got bored with the dinosaurs and went to look at the Mexican Indian ex-hibits down on the second floor. When I got back upstairs, he was talking to you."

I dabbed at my eyes again. "Well, that part worked out all right. But . . . but today, don't you see, I was supposed to come here to the museum with him and I was supposed to stay with him the whole time. But instead I left him at the entrance and then I w — w — went back home."

"Yes," Johann said softly. "Why did you? Why did you go back?"

I couldn't bear to look at Johann. "Be-cause of my *hair*," I suddenly shrieked, clos-ing my eyes and clapping both hands to my head in self-anger. "Because of this stupid, ridiculous, insane, crazy head of — "

I stopped short. An alarming thing had happened. My hair had dried at last in the warm, humid air, and again it had frizzed out into a thousand finely curled snarls and corkscrews. It must have been standing nearly six inches away from my head in all directions and looking every bit as impos-sible as it had early that afternoon when I'd left Arthur at the museum and gone back to the apartment to rewash it.

Suddenly, I broke out into wild laughter. Johann looked at me in alarm and offered me his hand to pull me up from the step on which I was still sitting. "I see nothing wrong with your hair, Tina. In fact, I think it is lovely. At home, where I come from, most of the girls have such thin, straight hair, it looks as though it had been manufactured out of long threads of nylon. It has no life of its own."

I glanced at Johann helplessly as, still holding my hand, he solemnly led me down the steps to the street. I felt too ashamed to tell him that I'd actually gone back to the apartment to wash my hair all over again. And, besides, he'd said he liked — actually liked — my hair.

"Which way do we go, Tina?" Johann asked me when we reached the corner. I pointed the way, and we started to walk westward toward the next avenue. Johann wasn't holding my hand now, but I was walking close beside him like a sleepwalker, still clutching the handkerchief he'd given me.

We came to the drugstore, with the display of hand mirrors in the window, where Arthur and I had stopped on our way over to the museum. Johann was looking at his wristwatch. "It's growing very late, Tina. Do you mind if we stop here for a moment so I can telephone my father or leave a message at the hotel desk if he's not there?"

"No, of course I don't mind."

I stood a short distance from the phone booth in the drugstore while Johann dialed the number. While it was still ringing, he turned to me. "Tina, I've just thought of it. You, too, must phone your parents from here. Right away. They will be worrying about you terribly." Then someone answered and he spoke into the receiver.

A minute later, he hung up. "It's all right. He's having dinner with business acquaintances. I'm to have mine alone at the hotel restaurant this evening. Now" — he stepped out of the booth and waved me into it with his hand — "you must call up your parents at once."

I hung back. Johann, of course, didn't even know how many parents I had. Not only were there Mom and Pop, there was Peter, who really could and should be considered a parent. There was Nana Tess, who wasn't just a grandmother but was some kind of a superparent, and there was even . . . even going to be Rosebud, heaven forbid, one of these days.

"Oh, I can't, Johann," I protested. "What would I say to them? 'I've lost Arthur'?" I covered my face with my hands. "No! It's too terrible."

Johann placed his hands on my shoulders and looked into my eyes. "Tina, at this point they think that *both* of you are lost. Have you ever thought of that? You must let them know that you, at least, are all right. They will be grateful to hear it. Believe me."

I honestly hadn't thought of that. And also, it was probably better not to wait any longer to let them know about Arthur. If the police had to be notified — well, the sooner the better.

I had to think for a moment, in the middle of all my confusion, to remember the number. Then, my finger shaking and my whole face twitching, I dialed.

There was only one ring, cut short as though somebody was standing beside the phone waiting. The receiver was picked up, and I heard Mom's voice, sounding thick and low-keyed.

"Yes?"

"It's Tina," I whispered hoarsely.

"It's Tina," I could hear Mom repeating to someone beside her or behind her. "Tina, where in the world have you been so long? We were actually beginning to worry."

Beginning to worry? What was that supposed to mean? Didn't they realize how late it was, or didn't they know what time the museum closed?

"I'm . . . uh . . . we're on the way home from the museum now." I turned to Johann who was standing anxiously beside me. "W–with a friend. Johann. You know — the boy we were talking about yesterday?"

"Oh, that's nice," Mom said. "Maybe he can stay and have supper with us."

"But . . . but listen. I have to tell you about Arthur — " My voice was trembling. How could I go on? There was a long stretch of silence at both ends of the line.

After a while, Mom said, "What *about* Arthur? What did he do now?"

"Well — ah, nothing. That I know of," I answered shakily. "It's just that Johann and I have looked everywhere, and we've tried all through the museum, and we — can't *find* him anywhere. Not any — w — w — where!"

I'd barely managed to choke out my last words when they were drowned in my own sobs and gulps, so intense that my ears seemed to close up completely and I couldn't hear anything Mom was saying in response.

The man who ran the drugstore and who had tried to sell me the brand of shampoo I didn't want raced around from behind the counter and peered at me in alarm, and Johann took the phone from my hand and began talking to Mom.

I sat collapsed on the little seat attached to the wall in the phone booth, my face masked in Johann's white handkerchief, which was rapidly becoming wet enough to wring out. "Arthur's gone and it's my fault. Arthur's gone and it's my fault." Those were the only words I could think of. My world was going round and round in a dizzying downward spiral.

I had no idea how long Johann went on talking to Mom or what they were saying. After a while, though, I heard the receiver being put back on the wall with a decisive slam. Johann's finger plucked at the corner of the handkerchief covering my face. I drew it away in silent terror.

"Tina," Johann commanded, "stop worrying. It's all right."

I looked up at him through wet, blurry eyes and completely fogged glasses. "What do you mean?" I blubbered. " 'It's all right'?"

"It's all right," he exclaimed, smacking his hands together noisily in delight. "It's all right. Arthur's found! Actually he's never been lost. He's at the apartment with your parents. They found him waiting on the doorstep of the building when they arrived home."

"What!"

"Yes, truly. He's been there with them for more than an hour."

"What was he doing waiting in front of the apartment building?"

"He went there to meet *you.*"

"To meet *me?*"

"Yes, it seems he was worried that you would have to get into the elevator alone when you went down to go to the museum to meet him, and this would be dangerous. So he thought that if he left the museum early he would reach the apartment before you left it. That's why he went so quickly from the Planetarium."

I clapped my hand to my forehead. "Oh, no! Oh, that Arthur. He's impossible! And what did he do when he got to the apartment building?"

"Well, it seems he found somebody to go up in the elevator with him. But the apartment was locked and you had already gone. To meet *him.* So then he went down again and simply waited. If he had tried to go back to the museum, you two would no doubt have missed each other again."

I stood up and blew my nose hard into Johann's handkerchief. "But I *told* him not to worry about me. Why couldn't he simply have followed instructions and waited in the museum? Now look what he's done."

We left the drugstore and started walking quickly toward home. "Don't be angry with him," Johann said softly. "He did it out of concern for you. He's very thoughtful and loving toward you, Tina. Just as the reason *you* came to the museum early was out of concern for him. I have no sisters or brothers, but if I did I should like them to be exactly this way."

"Still," I insisted, "Arthur should have waited where he was supposed to. What he did was really dumb. It caused all this trouble." I turned to Johann. "For you, too."

Johann laughed. "Would you believe me, Tina, if I told you that today has been one of the best days of my life?"

11

Arthur and I went back at Nana Tess's. Except Nana Tess herself wasn't back yet. She was due home from Greece in two more days, and school was going to begin a few days after that. Johann, of course, was back in Holland.

I didn't know when, or if, I'd ever see Johann again. He'd given me his address and I'd given him mine, and we'd agreed to write. But I couldn't even begin to think of what

I'd say to him in a letter, especially if I allowed myself to think of him as my "boyfriend," as Amy said he was.

I really preferred to think of him as my friend who was a boy, the first boy I'd learned to feel comfortable and normal and natural with. I suppose it took the crisis of Arthur's disappearance that afternoon for me to stop thinking of myself for once and to get to know and appreciate Johann for what he really was. After that, we had a wonderful time together. In fact, the whole world got much nicer.

I hoped the "glow" of my experience with Johann was going to last a while because now that I was back home I was really going to need it. Practically the only person that I was still talking to was Amy, and she'd gone away for the last week of summer, with her parents, on the Saturday morning right after the Friday evening of Karla's party.

Naturally, I was dying to know — well, curious anyway — about Karla's party. But I couldn't ask Ina, since we weren't speaking to each other anymore, and of course Karla was completely out of the question. So I was really pleased when Amy phoned up on the Sunday evening of the Labor Day weekend to say she was back home from visiting her grandmother in Virginia because her father didn't want to take a chance getting stuck in the holiday traffic on Monday.

"Come over, can't you?" I urged.

Amy groaned and yawned. "I'm really too tired, Tina. It was such a long drive. We left early this morning and just drove, drove, drove. I guess there's a lot to catch up with. If I can remember it all."

"Oh, Amy," I said, my heart sinking. "Isn't your memory ever going to improve? I'll just scream if you tell me you don't remember anything that happened last week."

"Oh, *I* remember, Tina," she answered with unexpected brightness. "For goodness' sake, you don't think I'd forget a thing like that. How is he, anyway?"

"He?" I asked. "Who do you mean?"

"Your boyfriend, silly. Joe. See I even remembered his name. And you thought that it was a good idea for my club name to be Amy the Amnesiac."

"Oh, say, Amy, that's pretty good . . ." I hesitated. "You really did remember his name. Joe, that is. He's fine, just fine. But listen, before I tell you any more about him, I think you should know that, as far as I'm concerned, the Saturday Sad Souls Club doesn't exist anymore. Well, at any rate,

I'm out of it. I think it was a pretty silly idea in the first place. I guess I'm allowed to say that because I'm the one who started it."

Amy sounded disappointed. "Oh, why? I kind of liked the club. We had fun at some of the meetings. You've got to admit that."

"Well, we *didn't* have fun at some of the others. At least, I didn't. And anyhow, that was nearly a year ago when the club began — and things change. I don't feel like being a Sad Soul anymore. Oh, I'm not going to try being one of those teen-model types either. I'm just going to try to be me. Not so critical of myself anymore or of anybody else either. It makes life too hard. Even though I don't think very much of Karla, I've got to admit she was right about one thing. We've got to start living our lives instead of just sitting around and talking about them."

Amy didn't say anything. She seemed to be thinking. Or maybe she'd fallen asleep altogether. Then, after a moment and sounding fairly wide awake, she said, "Speaking of Karla, I'm sorry I didn't call you up that Friday night right after the party."

At last she'd gotten around to Karla's party. But I didn't want to sound too anxious, so all I said was, "How could you have? It would have been too late."

"No, it wouldn't, Tina. We were back in my house by half-past nine. Ina and me, that is."

"Half-past nine?"

"That's right, Tina. We watched the rest of the party from the upstairs TV room, the same room where we had that meeting — I guess maybe the last meeting — of the SSSC. Remember?"

"Yes, I remember it well," I assured her. "But how come you and Ina left the party so early?"

Amy's voice was faint. She seemed to be fading out on me again. "We had to."

"Had to? But why? Was something the matter?"

"I s'pose you could say that. You see, it got kind of rough."

"Rough?"

"Well, yes. You know, Karla asked Tiger to bring a lot of friends, and she was supposed to invite the girls?"

"And?"

"And the way it turned out, Tiger brought along five boys and the only girls there were Karla and Ina and me.

"So?"

"So . . ." Amy paused and took a deep breath, trying to get a second wind. "Well, first the boys said they didn't like the food. It was mostly cheese and crackers because Karla's father forgot to get the charcoal for the barbecue grill and her mother forgot to buy the meat. Then they ran out of Coke and there was nothing else to drink. Karla had the music playing and we girls danced, but the boys didn't seem to want to. In fact, they just ignored us, especially Ina and me, until they got the idea to start jumping in the pool. . . ."

"Yes?" I said, listening intently.

"Pretty soon they started pushing one another in the pool. You know, climbing out and then shoving one another back in?"

"Um hmmm."

"Then they got the idea the girls should start jumping in the pool. They said if we didn't jump in they'd push us in."

"I see."

"They wanted Ina to jump in first. This was all down at the shallow end, of course. But she wouldn't. So then they said they'd push her in, and Ina started screaming. Karla told Tiger to make them quit teasing her, but they wouldn't. Ina was screaming like anything by then. I think she went hysterical.

Tiger tried to tell them to leave her alone, but I could see he had a grin on his face, too. They were pulling poor Ina around on the ground, and by that time even Karla and I were screaming. Finally, Ina managed to get up and she grabbed my hand, and we both ran across Karla's garden and through the hedge into my garden and got safely into our house through the back-porch door."

"Honestly, Amy," I said, after trying to visualize the whole scene, "I don't see what Ina was making such a fuss about. I thought it was *supposed* to be a swimming party."

"It was," Amy answered plaintively. "Only, Tina, there was no water in the pool. Karla's father never got around to having it cleaned out and filled up."

"Oh, I don't *believe* it!"

"Yes. Cross my heart, Tina. It's true."

It took me quite a while to digest the entire story. It seemed the party finally ended about a half hour later with Karla's brother coming out of the house and shooing everybody home. Karla's parents weren't even around. They were having dinner with some old friends in the city. It was really amazing how Amy had managed to remember so many details. She was turning out to be no more of an amnesiac than Karla was a klepto-maniac.

"Ina must have felt just terrible," I finally remarked. "I guess you both felt terrible."

"Oh," Amy said casually, "that's only half of Ina's troubles." She yawned. "Gee, I'm sorry, Tina. I'm just going to have to hang up and go to bed."

"Wait a minute, Amy," I gasped. "Just hang on another second. What's the other half?"

"Half? What other half?"

"The other half of Ina's troubles," I said, grinding my teeth. "You just said . . ."

"Oh, that. It's about her mother. You know that man who's been taking her mother out all summer? Well, her mother's going to marry him and Ina just hates the whole idea."

I quickly hung up the phone and let Amy go to bed. So my muttered curse had come true!

I woke up a couple of times during the night, and each time I thought of Ina being pulled around on the ground by Tiger's friends and, on top of that, having to face living with a whole new father. I had just gone through the same thing myself. Well, perhaps not exactly, because I wasn't going to be living with Peter and Mom all the time, even though Arthur and I would surely be going there for weekends a lot from now on. And the really big difference was that Peter had turned out to be just about perfect, even though I couldn't quite think of him as a father or love him in that way as much as I did Pop.

But there *was* a real problem that Ina and I shared. She had her Walter P. Drabble and I had . . . Rosebud. I'd been back home with Pop for two days now and I hadn't seen Rosebud yet. In fact, Pop hadn't mentioned her name since that day at the Flying Dolphin when I'd told him what I really thought of Rosebud. I would never have said all those things to him if I hadn't been so angry and upset at the time. I'd just had the fight with Ina, and she'd accused me of not being able to "stand" the truth. Anyhow, I guess Pop thought it would be better to keep Rosebud in the background for a while.

Even before I was up and dressed the next morning, I knew I was going over to Ina's first thing after breakfast. When I came downstairs to the kitchen, Arthur was sitting at the breakfast table, all sleepy and tousled, still in his pajamas, leaning on one elbow and eating some kind of perfectly terrible chocolate-flavored breakfast cereal with milk. Nellie, who had come in early to get the house straightened up for Nana Tess's return, was already running the vacuum cleaner in the living room.

Arthur looked up in shock. "What are you doing all dressed up so early? We don't have to go to the airport until three o'clock. Pop only just left to play tennis at the club."

"I'm not dressed *up*," I said. "I'm just dressed. I have to go over and visit a friend I haven't seen for a while."

"Oh," Arthur said, seeming satisfied. He stirred his dry cereal around listlessly. "Gee, Teen, don't you wish we had some of Peter's hot banana waffles for breakfast right now? Remember the time he put chocolate chips in them? I asked Nellie and she said she never heard of such nonsense. What nonsense? If I had some sliced bananas to put in this chocolate cereal, it would be the same thing. More or less. But of course it wouldn't taste as good."

"Arthur," I pleaded. "Please stop it. I'm trying to get down a simple glass of milk and a piece of raisin toast, and I don't think I'm going to make it."

My stomach was jumping. Suppose Ina

refused to see me? Or she came to the door and slammed it in my face? Still, something was pulling me straight to her house. I just had to do it — try to see her, tell her how sorry I was about everything, and hope that we'd be friends again.

I decided to walk over to Ina's rather than ride my bike. It was a nice day, not too hot out yet, and very quiet and hushed along the tree-lined streets with their early-morning lawns sparkling in the sun. When I got to Ina's house, I went up the front walk with my knees wobbling and rang the bell. Luckily it was Mrs. Philips who answered the door. She was wearing a long, frilly white robe dotted with small sprigs of violet-colored flowers. Her hair was dyed a new color, more honey-gold than red, and she looked very cheery and happy to see me.

"Tina, Tina, Tina," she said, thrusting out both her hands and practically pulling me over the doorstep. "Come right in. It's lovely of you to drop over. I guess you heard the good news. My girls are going to have a father again. It's quite, quite wonderful. Don't you agree?"

"Oh, yes," I said looking around the entrance hall and trying to peer into some of the other rooms. There seemed to be big bouquets of flowers all over — Mr. Drabble's courting, no doubt — but no signs of Ina anywhere.

"Congratulations," I murmured. "That's what I came over for. I thought I'd . . . congratulate you . . . and uh, Ina, too, of course."

Mrs. Philips tried to put her arm around my shoulders but quickly dropped it to my waist. She was a couple of inches shorter than I was. Her voice softened to a whisper. "I'm so glad you've come, Tina dear. Ina's still in her room, but I'll go up and tell her you're here. You know, she's still getting used to the idea. I keep telling her it's going to be the best thing for all of us. What's done is done. It's time to forget the cold, unfeeling hearts of the past. Just as they've forgotten us."

I nodded, and Mrs. Philips started up the stairs. I stood uncertainly near the front door, just in case Ina let out a furious scream and I had to bolt out of there in a hurry.

An awfully long time seemed to go by. I listened for the sound of voices, but I couldn't hear any. After a while, Mrs. Philips came to the top of the staircase and leaned over the banister.

She was still whispering. "You can come up now, Tina." I wondered how much Mrs.

Philips knew about our fight. Or maybe it wasn't that at all. In fact, it was beginning to sound like Ina was sick or something. I climbed the stairs nervously, as though I was on my way to visit somebody in a hospital.

The door of Ina's room was open, and she was puttering around in her pajamas and bare feet. She had a brush in her hand and was looking into the mirror, trying to do something with her hair. When she turned around, I could tell right away that she'd been crying.

"Oh, Ina," I said, rushing forward. I really wanted to put my arms around her, but she looked so red-eyed and sullen. And I didn't want to embarrass her. "I'm sorry," I gulped. "About . . . our fight and all sorts of things. I said an awful lot of rotten things to you that day. Some . . . some of th–them, you didn't even hear."

I could hear the door close softly behind me. Mrs. Philips must have gone back downstairs.

Ina sat down on the vanity-table bench, her legs sprawled in front of her and the hairbrush dangling in her hand. I sat down on the rumpled bed opposite her.

She swung the brush back and forth. "Oh,

let's forget it, Tina," she mumbled, not looking up. "I guess we both said a lot of nasty things. It wasn't worth it, of course. Karla's party was just awful. Awful! I wish it had never happened."

"I know," I said. "Amy described it to me. You know, for a so-called amnesiac, she certainly remembered . . . well, just about everything that happened. I guess nobody sees much of Karla these days."

"Oh, she floats around," Ina said numbly. "She's always meeting new people and getting very enthusiastic over them. Like she did about us."

"Well," I said, still feeling my way cautiously, "I suppose that's Karla's way of handling her problems. She must have problems, or she wouldn't have lied and said she was a kleptomaniac just to get into the Saturday Sad Souls Club. I guess Amy told you all about that — I mean about her *not* being a kleptomaniac."

"Yes." Ina nodded, still focusing on the hairbrush. Then she looked up at me, really looked at me for the first time. "So you're back," she said. "Did you have a real good time in the city?"

"I honestly did, Ina," I said. "Everything worked out so much better than I thought it would. My mother's new husband turned out to be a wonderful person. He's just like a good friend. We like him so much, both Arthur and me." Ina was staring down at the hairbrush again. I touched her wrist. "Listen, Ina, I just know things are going to work out fine with your mother and . . . and Mr. Drabble, too."

Ina shook her head, refusing to look up. "They're getting married at Christmas," she said. "That's only a few months from now. He took us all out to dinner at his club last night: my mother and the twins and me. And he formally announced that he was going to be our father. We're supposed to call him Papa Wally, on account of his first name's Walter. You remember. Walter P. Drabble?"

"Yes," I said solemnly. I still couldn't help feeling guilty about having wished her mother would marry Mr. Drabble, even though I was sure now that Ina hadn't heard what I'd said.

"Try thinking of it this way, Ina," I said earnestly. "Sometimes when parents have these problems with divorce and remarrying, you get kind of angry at them. They just don't seem to be playing their part right. I was pretty annoyed with my mother for a long time. In fact, I'm still not completely

191

over it. But it's lots better than it used to be. I'm really getting to like her now, as a person. And somehow it all sort of makes me feel more grown up."

Ina simply nodded.

"And in the case of your mother, well, it's really been hard for her, worrying all the time about money and how to keep up the mortgage payments on the house. You said yourself she'd become a nervous wreck since your father left."

Ina jerked her head in another nod.

"So won't it be nice for her to be calmed down and relaxed for a change? I'm sure she'll be a lot easier to live with. And then you'll be happier, too. Maybe you'll even stop being an insomniac and needing all those midnight snacks."

Ina glanced up. "I wonder if that might actually happen. I really ought to start losing some weight. It's that eating at night that's killing me. Like I told you."

"Of course," I said. Ina ate plenty in the daytime, too, but there was no sense going into that. If she stopped eating at night, she would be cutting down by nearly fifty percent. Which would certainly be a big help. "And as for Mr. Drabble," I went on, "he may turn out to be a lot nicer than you think.

Just remember, looks aren't everything. Or age. You have to get past those . . . barriers to . . . to really know a person." I suppose I was thinking about Peter . . . *and* Johann. "At least Mr. Drabble's willing to take care of you all. You don't have to think of him as a father if you don't want to . . . just as a nice person who came to live with your family. And likes you well enough to take the responsibilities of a father."

Ina sighed. I could see she still wasn't convinced, but maybe she felt just a tiny bit better. "Well, anyhow," she said, after another sigh, "it'll be nice us being friends again, Tina. And maybe you *will* be able to help me get adjusted. I always did think you were the most sensible one among us."

"Me?" I said. "Really?"

Maybe that was what Johann had meant when he'd told me, a couple of days after Arthur was "found," that all along he'd been thinking I was about fourteen. I guess it was the most flattering thing he ever said to me. Of course, I told him the truth — that I wasn't even thirteen yet, only short of half past twelve. But, by then, it didn't make a bit of difference to him.

I figured it was time for me to leave. I got up off Ina's bed. "I think I'll go home now, Ina, and take a swim before lunch. We have to go to the airport this afternoon to meet my grandmother's plane. She's coming back from Greece. I guess you knew."

"I heard," Ina said, walking me to the door of her room. "Who's going to the airport with you and your father? Is *she* going?"

I turned and looked at Ina sharply. "You mean Rosebud, don't you? I don't know. I haven't said a word to Pop about her since I'm home, and he hasn't said a word to me. I thought maybe if I didn't talk about her she'd go away. But I don't know."

I opened the door in Ina's room and began to skip down the stairs. "Call for me the first day of school, Ina. We'll go together. But I'll talk to you on the phone before that."

When I got to the bottom of the stairs, I looked up. Ina was leaning over the banister and shaking her head. "I wish you luck, Tina, about you-know-what." She wasn't saying Rosebud's name, I guess, because she didn't want her mother to know what we were talking about. "But take it from me, it'll never work out the way you want it to. Once they make their minds up, that's that."

"I'll see," I said. "I'll let you know."

Suddenly I was in an awful hurry to get home and find out.

12

We were sitting in the lobby of the terminal building at the airport, waiting for the "delayed arrival time" of Nana Tess's flight from Greece to be posted. Being the end of the last big holiday weekend of the summer, the sky was probably thick with planes. We'd already been waiting for over an hour, and Arthur, of course, had started to get hungry and gone to the snack bar to buy himself a hot dog.

I turned to Pop. "Too bad we didn't know the plane was going to be this late. You could have played a few more sets of tennis this morning . . . with Rosebud." It was the first time I'd mentioned her name to him since my outburst — and it took some doing.

Pop smiled. "Right. Well, I didn't want to wear the poor girl out too much." He paused and shook his head. "Although she's a powerful player with fantastic stamina. She doesn't get worn out easily, let me tell you."

I turned my eyes away in despair. Ina was probably right. Once they make their minds up . . .

Pop followed my gaze. "You hungry too, Sunflower?" He started to reach in his pocket. "Want to go get yourself something to eat?"

"Uh-uh," I said. "I'm not hungry in the least." I turned back to Pop. "How come Rosebud didn't come with us this afternoon to meet Nana Tess? She's practically part of the family now, isn't she? You and she did say you were going to get married in September, didn't you?"

Pop uncrossed his legs, then recrossed them, and folded his arms. He was more tanned and handsome than ever and was wearing a dark-blue blazer with brass buttons, an open-collared shirt, and a dark-red silk-print ascot at his neck. He cleared his throat.

"I've been meaning to talk to you, Sunflower, about Rosebud. And to Arthur, too."

I glanced over toward the snack bar. "There's a very long line over there. He might not be back for twenty minutes. Or more."

Pop nodded and cleared his throat a second time. "Well, I guess I do owe you an explanation. After all, you were honest with me that day when you called Rosebud a 'phony.' "

I glanced at Pop nervously, but he just kept looking straight ahead.

"So I decided to be honest with myself," he went on, "and I took a long, careful look at the situation. And guess what I found out?"

"What?" I asked anxiously.

"I found out that *I* was the phony."

"You?"

Pop turned to me. "Yes, me. Yours truly. I was being as phony as a four-dollar bill."

"Why? I don't understand."

"Because my reasons for thinking I wanted to marry Rosebud were all wrong. The very last reason you should marry someone is because you feel sorry for them."

I wrinkled my forehead. "You were feeling *sorry* for Rosebud? But why? She seemed to have everything going for her."

Pop took my hand. "Appearances are deceptive, Sunflower, as I think you're finding out these days. Rosebud has had more troubles than you or I will ever know. She had to run away from the country she was born in and leave her home, her family, her friends, almost everything behind."

"I know," I said, "but what about her money? Her Swiss bank account. She's rich anyway, isn't she?"

Pop shook his head. "I'm *in* the banking business, Tina, so it's hard to fool me about things like that. Actually, Rosebud's bank account was mostly wishful thinking, I'm afraid. She had a little money, just enough to get over here and buy the right clothes, join the right country club, and meet the right people, mainly so she would wind up marrying some 'rich American.' I knew exactly what she was up to and I thought maybe I'd help her out, let her dream come true. I suppose I even liked the idea of marrying someone who really needed me. You see, it was rough on me when I found out that your mother ... didn't."

Pop fell silent.

"Oh — h — h — h," I said, leaning forward and staring hard at the lobby floor, which was made up of tiny, many-sided white tiles. "That's quite a story. Does that mean you decided not to marry her?"

Pop nodded. "Yup. I gave her some good advice instead, about investing some of the money she had left in a small business — a boutique dress shop — in just the right part of town. Even negotiated a very low-interest loan for her through our bank. She and I will still be friends, of course. We make good tennis partners. But as to marriage partners . . ." Pop shook his head. "That idea is finished. I figure everybody'll be a lot happier that way."

I turned to Pop and threw my arms around him. "Oh, I *love* you!" I exclaimed. Pop hugged me back hard.

"What's wrong with you two? Is Tina feeling sick or something? Are you about to throw up, Teen?"

It was Arthur, standing in front of us with a limp hot dog, resting on a limp roll, the whole thing slathered over with mustard and cascading with sauerkraut. "Because I just brought you something to eat. But of course if you don't want it, Tina, I'll eat it myself."

Today feels like the first day of my life. . . .

For one thing, it was the first day of school. Ina and I went together, and during the break between second and third periods, guess who we should see coming down the corridor toward us but Tiger Rawson. He was with two other boys.

Ina let out a gasping screech and ducked into the open doorway of a classroom we were just passing. It all happened so fast that I didn't have time to do anything. Suddenly Tiger was right up close to me. He didn't grin very hard. In fact, he looked quite serious. And all he said as he passed and lifted his hand in a sort of half salute was, "Hello, Tina."

"Hi," I said back. I guess it was the first time I'd ever had anything to do with Tiger that my nose didn't twitch.

It was absolutely right, I decided then and there, that the Saturday Sad Souls Club should be disbanded. Amy wasn't an amnesiac anymore, Ina wasn't going to be an insomniac for much longer, Karla had never been a kleptomaniac in the first place, and I — Tina — had actually gotten past an encounter with Tiger Rawson without a single twitch.

Ina crept out from behind the doorway. "Wow," she breathed, "that was close. I'm sorry, Tina. There just wasn't time to warn you. What did he say to you? Was it awful?"

"No," I replied. "All he said was 'Hello, Tina.' It wasn't awful. In fact, it didn't hurt a bit."

The third and most important "first" thing happened when I got home from school this afternoon. Nana Tess, who came back from Greece with her skin tanned walnut-brown and her dark eyes snapping and dancing, was standing on a stepladder in the front hallway. She had bought out the souvenir shops of four or five Greek islands, to say nothing of the mainland. Everything had been an "exceptional bargain," of course, and when I came in the door, she was busy hanging up one of those brightly-colored, hand-woven Greek wool rugs, on the wall beside the staircase.

"There's something waiting for you up in your room, Miss Tina Carstairs," she remarked drily.

I looked at her oddly. She had never called me *that* before. I brushed past her quickly and up the stairs to my room. And there on the desk I saw it — my very *first* letter from Johann.

I don't know why exactly, but my name written in his handwriting, the foreign stamps in the corner, and the slanting red-and-blue airmail stripes all around the pale-blue, tissue-thin envelope made my heart thump furiously. I picked up the envelope with trembling fingers, tore it open as carefully as I could, and read the letter.

I still don't know when I'll see Johann again. He says that maybe he'll be able to come back again next summer. Or possibly — just possibly — at Christmas. But no matter what happens, we will keep on writing. And even if we don't ever see each other again, I know that he'll always be the most important thing that happened to me last summer — the most telltale summer of my entire life. So far.

About the Author

Lila Perl has been writing for years. She has had all different types of books published—from cookbooks for adults to fiction for young readers. Her books include, *No Tears For Rainey, Me and Fat Glenda, That Crazy April*, and *Dumb Like Me, Olivia Potts*.

Lila Perl lives in Beechhurst, New York and says of writing, "I love it with a passion." She answers every single fan letter that she receives.